Winning a Cowgirl's Love

Stephanie Berget

Winning a Cowgirl's Love
Copyright © 2018 Stephanie Berget
All rights reserved.

Other Titles by Stephanie Berget

Sugar Coated Cowboys

Gimme Some Sugar

Sweet Cowboy Kisses

Cowboy's Sweetheart

Sugar Pine Cowboy

Sugar Coated Cowboys Series-Box Set

Change of Heart Cowboys

Radio Rose

Rodeo Road

Changing A Cowboy's Tune

Copper Mills World

Silver Dreams…On a Tin Can Budget

STEPHANIE BERGET

DEDICATION

To my good friend and writing partner, D'Ann Lindun. You've given me so many opportunities, so much great advice, and so many good books to read. Thanks for everything, cowgirl.

And, thanks to Jessica Joslin for allowing me to use your wedding photo on the cover of this book. You're the poster girl for all the cowgirl brides out there.

STEPHANIE BERGET

CHAPTER ONE

"I'd have to be the most gullible person on the face of the earth to believe you this time. I'm not that stupid, Christina." Randi Bachmann stood with her hands on her hips, glaring at her beautiful, pushy younger sister.

"Of course you're not, but . . ."

She cut Christina off mid-sentence with a wave of her hand. "I know you've always thought you were smarter than Cammie and me, and I know you think I'm the original country bumpkin. I know it makes your day to pull one over on me, but I'm not falling for your stupid prank." As Randi watched, the corners of her sister's mouth quivered with the effort not to smile.

It was time to leave.

"You aren't listening." Christina flipped her perfect blonde hair over one shoulder. She moved to block the way as Randi walked toward the door of the condo.

"I'm not kidding, Tina. I've had enough!" As Christina reached toward her, Randi tucked her fingers into the back pockets of her jeans to keep from being pulled into a dance around the coffee table. "This hasn't been my best year. I lost my horse to colic, I'm unemployed, and I haven't had a serious date in so long, I don't remember how it's done. Now is not the time for another of your practical jokes." She opened the door of Christina's expensive Boise condo and hurried outside.

Racing down the stairs, she climbed into her battered Ford pickup. The exterior was shabby, but it always ran. As the engine roared to life, she looked over her shoulder to check before backing onto the road.

Before Randi could get the gearshift rammed into reverse, Christina climbed into the passenger seat. "I'm sorry about your job, and your horse. I'm even sorry about your date situation, but I'm trying to help."

Her sister meant well—most of the time—but everything came easy to Christina. Of the three sisters, Christina was the only natural blonde, the only one with a rich fiancé who adored her, and the only one who didn't have to watch her weight.

Randi didn't mind the hair color or the money, but she had to work not to let the weight issue come between them. Once Christina had learned to not scarf down sweets in front of Randi or their older sister, Camille, they'd decided to let her live.

Besides, she wouldn't trade her life, problems and all, for her sister's, not for all the money in Boise. Christina lived in luxury, paid for by her tech whiz fiancé, while she finished her doctorate in Psychology.

Randi struggled to pay the rent on a small acreage in Homedale, Idaho, with just enough room to keep her two horses. The fact that she lived close to her older sister and four-year-old niece was a plus she was thankful for every day.

"The job wasn't much, but I hate that the western store went out of business. They were good people, and I hate job hunting."

"William can find you something—"

Randi cut her off. "I can't see me working in an office, and neither could you. I'm pretty sure the other employees would complain about the horseshit on my boots and the mud in my hair."

"You've got a point there, so what I'm trying to tell you is doubly important."

"Christina, I have things to do." Randi watched as a plethora of emotions raced across her sister's immaculately made-up face—annoyance, excitement, and hope, with excitement winning out in the end.

Christina reached out and laid her hand on Randi's arm. "You need to hear me out. You'll thank me."

"I doubt that. Look, if you don't get out, William will get his fancy new car all dusty when he has to come pick you up at my house, and you know that won't make him happy." Randi shifted into reverse and began backing out of the space in front of Christina's double-car garage.

Out of the corner of her eye, she saw Christina straighten. The impact of her sister's hand to the back of her head almost caused her to crash into a BMW coming down the street. She slammed on the brakes just in time.

"Miranda Evelyn Bachmann, listen to me!"

Randi turned toward her sister. The excitement was gone. The no-nonsense look that her little sister could pull off better than anyone she knew, had taken control. Randi pulled back into the driveway and turned off the key. "What!"

A smile crept across her sister's face. "You really did win the grand prize in the *Your Dream Wedding* Contest. You remember the one everyone was entering at the Bridal Show we went to last month? I entered you, and you won." She sat back with a cat-got-the-canary smile.

Randi's mouth dropped open, and it took a moment before she had the mental capacity to close it. She pulled in a deep breath and wedged her fingers between the back of her thighs and the seat to keep from grabbing her sister by her ears and shaking her. This joke had gone too far.

She hadn't had a steady boyfriend for over two years and hadn't been on a date of any kind for over six months.

She pulled in another breath, held it until her head

swam, and let it out slowly. When she'd managed to regain some control, she raised her gaze. "Why are you doing this? It isn't funny."

Christina's mouth twisted in an attempt to keep from smiling. "I'm not trying to be funny."

"I'm not engaged." Christina was well aware of that, but for some reason, Randi felt the need to tell her again. "I'm not getting married, therefore I don't need a wedding."

"I know." Her sister's exasperated sigh didn't help matters. "But you need money."

Randi laughed, but it was a hollow, defeated sound. Christina was talking in circles as usual, and after the way the last few months had gone, she didn't have the patience to figure it out. "Let me get this straight. I'm going to lie to the producers, marry a non-existent man, and run away with the wedding cake? I don't think there's a big market for used wedding cakes, and that's the only way I can see to make money from this scenario."

Christina leaned across the seat and pulled Randi into a hug. As they parted, she patted Randi's cheek a little harder than was necessary. "You silly girl. There's an all-expense paid wedding, anything you want, and there's—"

Randi cut her off. "I don't want any kind of wedding."

Christina opened the door and stepped out. She shut the door, but leaned in the open window. "I suppose you don't want the fifty thousand dollar bonus you'll receive if they get the wedding on film?"

"No, I don't."

Christina nodded, gave Randi a little wave, and strolled back to her house, her hair curling perfectly over the shoulders of her navy, beaded Oscar de la Renta blouse.

Randi put the truck in gear and drove home. In the hour it took to get there, she waffled between anger and sadness. When Christina had insisted Randi join her in San Diego for the biggest bridal show of the year, she'd reluctantly agreed. Tina's wedding was going to be a big event in Boise.

Even though Randi didn't think she'd be able to contribute, she'd flown down with her sister and tried to act happy. She did love her sister after all.

"You'll get ideas for your own wedding," Christina had said, over and over.

Why wouldn't the woman listen? If Randi ever did get married, which she wouldn't, it would be a quiet affair, probably in the county courthouse with only her best friend, Mavis, and Camille and Christina as witnesses.

Randi's cell phone rang. One glance told her it was Christina, so she hit mute and continued driving. She wasn't even going to get the little wedding, because she wasn't going to get married. Ever!

There had been a time when she'd made plans. Nothing as elaborate as her sister's, just something at the small chapel in Homedale with family and friends. She'd even hoped for the white picket fence and a couple of kids, but the pipedream was gone, along with the only man she'd ever loved.

She slapped her hand on the steering wheel until it stung and took her mind off weddings.

The phone rang again and again. She knew her pushy little sister. One time, in an attempt to ignore Christina she'd turned her phone off. When she'd turned it on the next day, she'd found twenty-three voice messages and thirty-two missed calls.

On the fourth call, she answered. "What?" Randi took the exit off the interstate and pulled into the parking lot at Whittenburger Park.

Christina's voice was all business now. "I know you're not going to get married right away. You've made that very clear, although you haven't told me why you're so put off by men. When I asked Mavis, she said you wouldn't tell her either."

"You talked about my love life with Mavis? That's none of your business." Randi laid her forehead against the steering wheel and sighed.

"And you're changing the subject. You're a smart, beautiful woman, and heaven only knows why you've picked losers to date the last few years—"

"Do you have a point, Tina?" Randi turned off the key and waited. It was times like this she wished she were an only child.

"I know you've saved for years to put a down payment on a place of your own." Christina was slightly out of breath, and Randi could hear traffic sounds in the background. Her skinny sister was jogging again. "I know you had one all picked out."

"That's one dream that's not going to happen." Tears filled Randi's eyes, and she tried to blink them back. She'd spent every last dime on her barrel horse. The surgery hadn't kept him alive, but she'd do it all over again in a heartbeat just for the chance to save him.

"Fifty thousand dollars, Randi. Five O." Christina's voice raised an octave or two. "You could get a nice place if you had that much money for a down payment."

Randi laid her head against the headrest and closed her eyes. Christina always shot for the moon. Funny thing was, she usually made it.

Randi had tried that method a couple of times and had fallen on her face. Her sister was one of those perennially lucky people. "Don't you think they'll get a little suspicious when I show up alone?"

"I haven't figured that part out yet, but I will. All I want you to do is think about this and keep an open mind."

Randi could imagine the smile on Christina's face even through the phone. "You mean keep an empty mind and let you take care of everything."

"Yes."

#

Davie Dunbar hoisted the newborn Hereford calf onto his saddle and mounted before the mama cow decided to take back her baby by force. The old girl was one of the new bunch his older brother, Dex, had bought at the sale. The girls weren't supposed to calve for several more weeks, but apparently this one moved to her own beat.

The little guy was tiny and shivering like an Aspen leaf. Davie rubbed one hand over the calf's ribcage then looked at the cow. "Come on, old girl. Let's get this handsome baby home."

As he pointed his horse toward the ranch house, he marveled at how many years he'd spent away from the Rafter D. The thing that surprised him most was how happy he was to be back in Eastern Oregon.

He topped the bluff overlooking the ranch buildings and made his way to the barn. Mama cow followed along behind, worrying and calling out to her calf in low, worried moos.

Just as he dismounted and put the calf on the ground in the corral, Mavis trotted up the driveway on her good mare, Tuneful. She dismounted and led the gray up to the fence. He had to admit, his brother had married a good woman.

"I see you found a new little one." Mavis slipped the bridle from her horse and pulled on a halter. "One of Dex's bargain cows?" She unfastened the breast collar then loosened cinches and tossed them across the saddle seat.

Davie waited until she'd stowed the saddle and blanket in the tack room of the barn before answering. "Yeah, this one didn't get the message they weren't supposed to calve yet."

They both leaned over the fence and watched as the little guy wavered on wobbly legs and began searching for his first meal. The old cow stood patiently until her calf was sucking away. The slurping noise made Mavis laugh. "I'll never get tired of that sight."

Davie's smile faded. He looked from the freshly

painted red barn to the faded out buildings. His grandfather had built most everything the year he and Nana Lucy had bought the ranch outside of Jordan Valley, Oregon. "There was a time when I thought I never wanted to see a cow or even Oregon again. I was wrong."

Mavis stood on her tiptoes and slung her arm over his shoulders. "We're sure glad you came to your senses. Dex is really happy you're back. Now if he could just get Drew to quit traveling all over the world."

Davie gave her a quick hug. "That's not going to happen. Not with superstar Chelsey's song climbing the charts."

For a moment, he thought he saw an angry look flash across his sister-in-law's face, but a small smile was there before he was sure. He'd never heard Mavis say anything against Drew's wife, but then he'd never heard her say anything against anybody. If he ever decided to marry, he was going to find a woman like Mavis.

He watched as his sister-in-law led her horse to a pen. Over her shoulder, a trail of dust rose from the road. Someone was visiting the Rafter D.

A faded red Ford pickup pulled up beside them, and Drew groaned. Randi Bachmann was in the house, and he hadn't had time to hide.

The brunette climbed out of the truck and peered through the fence at the calf. The little creature bounced around his mama, only making it a half-inch off the ground. "He thinks he's a bucking bull, doesn't he?" She turned to smile at Mavis, but when she caught sight of Davie, the grin faded to disgust.

It was probably disgust, but it could have been despair or even dejection. Davie wasn't sure which, because it quickly changed to anger. She turned her back on Davie and spoke to Mavis. "I wanted to talk to you about something, but it can wait. I'll see you later."

The wind picked up and lifted a lock of brown hair that had worked its way out of the long braid hanging down

Randi's back. Except for the summer after their first year in college, a braid had been her go to hairstyle. For those few months before everything had fallen apart, she'd turned the thick molasses colored curls loose.

As the strand of hair curled around her face, a memory flashed unbidden into his mind. Randi, her hair feathered across the pillow, just before they made love. Davie's breath caught in his lungs, and he was afraid his heart might stop beating.

For a moment, he had the urge to pull out the leather thong she used to keep the plait in place and run his fingers through her hair.

Sure, and lose his hand, because if he touched her, she'd take his arm off before he could react.

During the few times he'd seen her since college, she'd ignored him—unless he made her mad. He was unsure of what to say, so he fell back on his go-to strategy—sarcasm. "Need some advice? Doctor Davie's right here with all the answers."

Mavis' soft laugh did nothing to assuage the angry expression on Randi's face. Her brows drew together and her lips thinned into a frown, as a red flush worked its way up her neck to her cheeks.

Mavis touched her arm. "Randi?"

Randi froze for a moment before smiling at her friend. When she turned back to Davie, the anger had changed to scorn. "I think I'd rather be doused in honey and tied over an ant hill in the blazing sun before taking anything from you."

He managed to paste a grin on his face, and he thought he did a passable job of looking unaffected by her words. "You don't know what you're missing."

She'd started toward her truck, but at his words, she whirled. "Leave me alone, Davie!"

Mavis looked from one to the other.

Randi took a deep breath and let it out slowly. She shrugged her shoulders and relaxed marginally. "Davie," she said, her voice ridiculously soft and sweet and so totally unlike her it made him shiver. "I need to talk to Mavis. Can you excuse us?"

When he looked at Mavis, she gave him a barely perceptible nod. She looked as confused at Randi's attitude as he was—except he wasn't confused at all. He knew exactly why Randi hated him, and he didn't blame her a bit. He'd been young and stupid and scared, but all those reasons put together didn't justify what he'd done.

He widened his smile and made a point of looking Randi in the eye as he leaned toward her. "You know I'd do anything for you." He kept his voice a whisper. She wouldn't believe him yet, but maybe someday he'd be able to make things right.

Her frown deepened.

His unexpected words had shocked her into silence, so it was time to make his exit. Davie turned to Mavis. "I'll make lunch. Come on in when you're ready. Invite your friend, too." Without looking at Randi again, he made his way to the house.

After scrubbing his hands in the old, cast iron sink in the back room, he walked into the kitchen. Normally, his Nana Lucy would have had lunch ready, something hot and delicious.

Today, she was in town for a meeting of the Cowbells. Many of the rancher's wives and mothers belonged to the club, and they were planning their annual baked goods fundraiser. As a kid, he'd always loved the week before the bake sale. Nana would make tons of breads, cakes, and cookies. The ones she deemed not good enough, the boys got to eat.

Who was he kidding? As an adult, he loved this week.

He loaded the counter with last night's roast beef, cheese, and homemade bread and began putting together sandwiches. When he'd finished, he put a scoop of Nana's potato salad on each of three plates.

By the time he'd poured three glasses of ice tea, he

heard Mavis come through the back door.

"No Randi?" He'd known she wouldn't voluntarily spend time with him, but on the off chance she did decide she could eat lunch with the man she'd deemed the devil, he'd made a plate.

After washing up, Mavis sat at the table and picked up half of the overstuffed sandwich. "She had to get back home." Her eyes narrowed as she looked at him, and she laid the sandwich back on the plate. "What's going on between you two?"

Davie concentrated on his potato salad. After swallowing, he shrugged. "Don't know. I can't have made her mad. I haven't been in the same state for over five years."

"Something's going on. Randi's outspoken to say the least, but she doesn't treat people like that without cause."

"Maybe she's having a bad day." After he shoveled another bite of the salad into his mouth, he glanced up at Mavis. She was watching him with the look he'd seen her give Dex.

The *you'd-better-tell-me-the-truth-or-else* look.

While his brother had to keep her happy, Davie didn't. He'd do almost anything to keep from hurting his sister-in-law's feelings, but some things were private. If Randi hadn't told her best friend how he'd screwed up their relationship, he wasn't about to discuss their ill-fated love affair.

Davie grabbed his sweat-stained straw hat and what was left of his sandwich and hurried out the door before Mavis could grill him further.

He pulled the door shut then swung it open just far enough to stick his head back into the kitchen. "Sorry to eat and run, but I promised Dex's bargain cows we'd have an in-depth talk about parenting this afternoon."

STEPHANIE BERGET

CHAPTER TWO

Randi pulled a large Coke bottle from the ancient refrigerator. "Not that it's anybody else's business, but there isn't anything going on between Davie and me." She raised her voice so Mavis could hear her from the living room.

The doors from the upper cabinets were scattered around the miniscule kitchen, looking not quite as ratty in their new coat of bright white paint.

The first year she'd lived here, Randi hadn't done much fixing up. To be honest, she hadn't done anything. The one bedroom house on a half-acre had only been a stopping off place until she'd socked away the down payment for a home of her own. After searching for over a year, she'd found the perfect place.

She'd been three days away from signing the papers to make the small farm her own when her young barrel horse, Butter, had developed a bad case of colic. The nest egg she'd so carefully saved had vanished in less than a day.

She'd only owned Butter for a little over a year, but she'd loved him. To watch him suffer as Doc Percifield had tried to save his life had been almost too much to bear. Despite the Vet's best efforts, the operation hadn't

19

been a success, and with a heavy heart, she'd made the decision to let him go.

Randi swiped at the tears filling her eyes and poured two glasses of soda. She'd worked off some of her grief sanding and painting the walls and cabinets in the small kitchen, but apparently not all of it. With no money to move, it looked like she'd be here for quite a while longer. She had three more rooms to refurbish. Hopefully, by the time she finished, she'd be ready to look for another prospect.

"You've made it clear Davie's not your favorite person, but it's not like you to be nasty to anyone." Mavis moved to the archway separating the two rooms and leaned against the wall. "I don't think he deserved to be treated that way. Now what's going on?"

You don't know what Davie deserves. Randi almost broke down and spilled her biggest secret, but she snapped her mouth shut. She wasn't ready for anyone to know about the baby yet. Her kind-hearted friends would feel sorry for her, and she didn't deserve their pity.

After pouring the coke into ice-filled glasses, Randi handed one to her friend. "I'll watch what I say from now on. Now, tell me. How did you and Tuneful do at the rodeo last Saturday?"

As Mavis settled back onto the pickle green, Naugahyde couch, Randi busied herself wiping at the smudge on the old maple coffee table. When silence continued to fill the room, she looked up.

Mavis sat with her elbow on her knee, her chin in her hand, and a frown on her face.

"What?" While Randi didn't lose her cool very often, right now she was having trouble containing her anger. "Didn't I give you a good enough answer? Davie Dunbar has the spine of a snake and the morals of a skunk. If I never saw him again, it wouldn't bother me a bit, and while I wouldn't dance at his funeral, I wouldn't be very sorry either."

Mavis took a long swallow of Coke and leaned back against the couch. A smile crept across her face. "So, no feelings for Davie then?"

After a moment, Randi joined in her friend's laughter. She'd spent years keeping her feelings for Davie hidden from the world. "One day, I'll tell you, but I'm not ready yet."

"Fair enough." Mavis sank back into the worn couch. "I think Davie's changed, if that means anything."

"It doesn't. Tell me about the rodeo." The sound of the unending blast of a car horn from outside the house caused Randi to start.

Glancing out the window, she saw her younger sister's cherry red Jaguar pull into the driveway. Whirling, she pointed a finger at Mavis. "It's Christina. Don't agree with a single thing she says, and don't say anything about Davie."

At Mavis' quizzical look, Randi attempted to grin, but tension probably pulled it into a grimace.

Randi stomped across the room, pulling the door open before her sister had a chance to knock.

Christina swept into the room, gave Randi a drive-by hug and headed for Mavis.

Camille waited until Christina had finished her grand entrance before stepping through the door. Her pleasant smile faded to concern as she put her arm around Randi's shoulders. "You okay with Christina's plan?"

"That would be a great big N. O." Randi replied.

"Sure she is." Christina plopped onto the couch beside Mavis and swept her fingers through her sleek blonde hair. "She's just too stubborn to admit I did a good thing."

Arguing with Christina was an exercise in futility, so Randi changed the subject. "Do either of you want a Coke?"

"Water, please." Christina grinned and waved a dismissive hand at Randi. "With ice and lemon and a half teaspoon of organic honey."

Camille sank into the ancient overstuffed chair. "Nothing for me, thanks."

Randi almost laughed out loud. The answers were typical of her sisters. One was the definition of high maintenance, and the other always went out of her way to make life easy for everyone else.

She had a freezer full of ice and a lemon left over from the lemonade she'd made a few days ago. She even had a jar of local honey, but with Christina going out of her way to make life miserable, catering to her sister was out of the question. "I have tap water and Coke."

After grinning at Christina, Randi turned to Camille. "Where is Hailey? I need a distraction."

"She's with her daddy today."

One more reason not to get married. Camille had thought Tom was the love of her life. And he was until life got difficult. As the smartest of the sisters, if she couldn't pick a good man, what chance did Randi have?

As she carried the water back to the living room, the jubilant tone of Christina's words stopped her in her tracks.

"She won! Now all we have to do is find her a fiancé. I've started a list."

Mavis' gaze flicked from Christina to Randi to Camille and back. When Mavis made eye contact with her a second time, Randi gave a little shake of her head.

The non-verbal communication system between Mavis and Randi had been firmly in place since grade school, and Randi was sure her friend would change the subject before Christina could get all wound up.

Mavis turned to Christina. "What did she win, exactly?"

A sigh the size of Oregon escaped Randi as she set the glass of water on the coffee table in front of the women. So much for her best friend having her back. Mavis' one question would give her younger sister all the encouragement she needed to keep pushing the stupid reality show wedding. *Too bad I can't gift this big to-do to*

Christina. All the flash and glitter is right up her alley.

Her eyes shining with excitement, Christina grabbed the glass, slopping some onto the couch. "Only the wedding of her dreams." She dabbed at the spill, all the while grinning like a loon.

"I don't dream, and I don't want a wedding." Randi wandered to the window and looked out at the small pasture. Her retired barrel horse, Drummer, stood head to tail with the rope horse she'd bought last year, their tails making short work of the flies. Multi-colored iris bloomed along the base of the old trees, and the iridescent blues and greens of a humming bird flashed as it sped by.

Maybe if she didn't turn around, Christina would take the hint and leave.

"Miranda, come take a look at this list and tell me which guy is your first choice."

She opened her mouth to tell her sister, once again, that a wedding was out of the question, when Mavis took the list and studied it. "The first two and the fourth one are too old, and the rest are either married or getting a divorce. Not the perfect candidates for a fiancé."

Randi's frown was so deep, her brows nearly met her nose as she stared at her erstwhile friend. What the heck? Was Mavis siding with her ever-pushy sister?

She looked at Camille, but her older sister only shrugged.

Turning on her heel, Randi strode through the kitchen, grabbed her coat from the peg by the back door as she swept by, and hurried out to the shed that doubled as a tack room.

Picking up a halter from beside the gate to the pasture, she caught Drummer and led him to the hitching rail. Time to escape the conniving trio before they pushed her into something she'd regret until the end of her days. She slipped on the halter then ran her fingers through his mane. Drummer had been her roping partner since she'd entered her first High School Rodeo.

Leading Drummer out the gate, she snapped the gate chain.

"It's okay. We'll find someone."

Randi whirled to see if the two women were making her the butt of a joke, but Christina's smile was open and honest. She should have known better. Christina would never knowingly hurt her, and Mavis was her best friend. Neither woman knew the extent of the pain she lived with and hid from everyone.

Randi sighed. "I don't want to get married." Her voice came out as a whisper instead of the strong statement she'd intended. "I know you're trying to help."

"But the money. You won't take any money from me, and you can't spend the rest of your life in this shack. This is a perfect way to pay off your remaining vet bills and get a down payment for a place of your own."

Mavis laid a hand on Randi's shoulder. "She's got a point."

"What if they find out? I don't want to go to jail for fraud." Randi grabbed a saddle blanket from the shed and spread it on Drummer's back. "This would be a lie."

"It's only for six months." Christina climbed the rail fence and smiled down. "No one in these things stays together. They just want a great show."

As Randi went to get her saddle, Mavis pulled the blanket off and hung it over the fence. She took Randi's arm and led her outside the shed. "I know Butter's death devastated you both monetarily and emotionally. Just think about this."

Randi looked from her sister to her friend. They were doing this out of love, she knew that, but the thought of going through with the deception made her want to throw up.

Randi sank to the ground and leaned against the hitching rail upright. She broke off a long blade of grass and tied a series of knots down the length. Drummer moved closer and whuffed a warm breath into her hair.

"Honey, we don't have to get back to them until next Monday," Christina said.

Randi jerked her head up and looked her sister in the eye. "Monday? Why didn't you say so? That gives us four whole days. And here I was worried we'd be under a time crunch."

#

The large pig-shaped soup tureen was filled to the top with steaming chicken and homemade noodles. Davie placed it in the center of the kitchen table on the lace tablecloth. Even though it was just Davie, Dex and Mavis, Nana Lucy always set the dinner table like they were having company.

The sound of laughing voices floated in from the barnyard, and within seconds Dex came in the back door, his arm around Mavis' shoulders. As they washed up at the large sink on the back porch, they got into a water fight.

"Children!" Nana put a basket of warm dinner rolls on the table before taking her chair.

Dex and Mavis hurried to their places, dripping water drops from their hair.

As Davie bowed his head for Nana's obligatory prayer, the scent of apple pie cooling on the counter made his mouth water.

When they'd all said Amen, he grinned at Nana. "Any woman I marry is going to have awesome cooking skills, Nana. I won't accept anything less than this kind of feast every day." Davie watched as his grandmother's cheeks pinkened.

Dex pushed a lock of Mavis' hair behind her ear then looked at his brother. "I don't know, Davie. Good cooks are hard to find. Mavis can't cook a lick."

Mavis slapped her husband's shoulder. "You can't cook either. It's a good thing we live here. We'd starve to death if we had to feed ourselves."

Davie filled his soup bowl and passed the soup ladle to his brother. "I don't have to worry about finding a cook, because I'm not getting married."

Mavis choked on a mouthful of soup. The warm, rich broth splattered on her sweatshirt, and a bit of noodle clung to her chin. Dex took her spoon from her hand as she tried to get her coughing under control.

Davie grinned. "It can't be that much of a surprise that I'm not getting married." He'd spent the last years traveling the country, working hard at not getting tied down.

"No, it's not a big surprise." Mavis grinned as she retrieved her spoon from her husband. "It's just that I spent the day with Randi. She must have said those very words a hundred times."

"She's thinking about marriage?" Damn, he hadn't meant to say that out loud. Davie busied himself shoveling bites of chicken and noodles into his mouth. The hot liquid burned the crap out of his tongue, but this was one conversation he didn't want to discuss with his family. He swallowed and looked at his brother. "What'd you get bought at the sale today?"

Dex gave him a confused look. "I didn't go. You knew that."

"Oh, yeah. I forgot."

Before Davie could think up another subject, Dex turned to Mavis. "Who said she was getting married?"

"You're not going to believe this, but Christina entered Randi in a drawing at the wedding show they attended last month. She won."

All three heads swiveled away from their respective bowls and toward Mavis. A sharp jab of regret hit Davie's heart.

Dex chuckled. "I bet that set Randi off all right."

"And you haven't heard the best part." Mavis laid her spoon on the table and took a drink of her ice tea. "There's a fifty-thousand-dollar grand prize for letting this company, *Your Dream Wedding*, follow the winners around and film the wedding and everything leading up to the ceremony."

It was Davie's turn to choke. "Holy shit!"

"She's got to do that," Dex said matter-of-factly as he buttered his third roll.

Davie shook his head. "That's a lot of money, but getting married is a permanent venture. I don't think it'd be worth it."

"She only has to stay married for six months." Mavis suddenly sat up straight. Pointing her finger at Davie, she frowned then shook her head and relaxed. "Doesn't make any difference. Fake wedding or not, the guy would have to be someone Randi trusted. If the fake groom backed out before the six months, she'd have gone through all this for nothing."

"I'd volunteer, but she'd kill me before the wedding, and I'm too young to die." Davie grabbed the last two rolls before Dex ate them all. "Besides, I don't see her doing this for all the money in the Northwest."

"It would get the poor dear out of her money problems." Nana opened the oven door and pulled out another pan of rolls. She tipped them into the basket and sat back down.

"That's the thing. She stills owes the vet over twenty-five hundred dollars. Every penny she'd saved to buy a place is gone. Even if she split the money with the guy, she'd be out of debt and have a good nest egg." Mavis carried her bowl to the sink and rinsed it out. "I'm off to the barrel race. I'll be late."

Davie was fishing the last noodle out of his bowl when Dex touched his shoulder. "Why don't you volunteer?"

Confused, Davie looked up. "For what?"

Nana Lucy whacked him across the back of the head in the way she'd done since they'd been kids. "Be the groom."

Davie ducked out of his chair and placed his bowl in

the sink, moving out of Nana's reach. "Why would I do that?"

"For the money. You've talked about buying some cows of your own. Twenty-five thousand would make a good start on a herd of registered Angus." Dex hurried toward the back door. "I'm going with Mavis."

Davie grinned at the way his brother followed Mavis around. There'd been a day when Dex was only interested in rodeoing, but his priorities had changed. When a vision of Randi walking down the aisle toward him played through his mind, he could understand his brother's change of mind.

Nana Lucy's voice pulled him out of his musings. "And to help Randi. You might fool everyone else, but something happened between you and that girl years ago. You might want to make things right."

"By marrying her?" When his grandmother nodded, he shook his head. "She wouldn't marry me for all the money in the world."

As Davie cleared the table, Nana filled the sink with hot soapy water and began washing the dinner dishes, stacking them in the drainer. The three boys, at Mavis' urging, had bought her a dishwasher for her birthday, but it sat in the barn. She'd said, the day she was too old to wash a few dishes, was the day they'd put her down like a crippled mule.

"She really hates me, Nana. It wouldn't work."

His grandmother turned slowly to face him, and the look on her face was filled with pity. "You've always been stubborn and willful, but I never thought you were stupid."

CHAPTER THREE

Sunshine filtered through the trees lining the gravel road in front of Randi's house. A barely-there breeze cooled her sweat-dampened skin. All the way home, Drummer had wandered along, his head swinging in time with his steps.

Unable to get her mind off the wedding she'd won, Randi had saddled her old horse and gone for a ride in the hills. She hadn't been able to make a decision, and the problem was no smaller, but from the back of a horse, she'd always been able to handle anything.

The money would be a life changer—but married? Potential disasters seemed to line up behind her at the thought. Besides, who would marry her?

There were any number of men who'd marry the money. She knew that. To even seriously consider a wedding, she'd have to find someone who wouldn't throw her under the bus. She'd spent most of the ride trying to think of someone she could trust and had come up empty handed.

As Drummer drew close to her house, she saw Mavis leaning against the front of her truck. She stepped down from the old horse and loosened his cinch. "Come up with the perfect candidate?" As of last night, Mavis hadn't come up with a sacrificial man either.

Randi tried to relax. Tomorrow would be Monday, and she wouldn't have to think about this anymore. Twenty-four more hours and she'd be in the clear.

Broke, but in the clear.

Mavis followed her to the back of the house and up to the shed. "As a matter of fact, I did."

The smug look on her friend's face made Randi take a step back. She pulled the saddle off her horse and carried it into the tack shed, buying herself a little time.

After turning Drummer into the small pasture, she walked to the back of the house where Mavis sat in a raggedy lawn chair. Randi sank onto the steps.

"Don't you want to know who?"

"No, I don't think I do." Randi watched as Drummer lowered himself slowly to the ground and attempted to roll. The old guy couldn't make it all the way over, so after a couple of tries, he stood and dropped to his other side.

Whatever worked.

"You do, you just don't want to admit it." When Randi didn't answer, Mavis cleared her throat. "Davie."

Randi had known this was coming. Her only saving grace was the fact that Davie was the only person on the face of the earth who'd be more against this farce than she was. "And you've discussed this with Davie? He's agreed?" Feeling safe in her judgment of Dex's brother, she played along.

"It was his idea." When Randi's head snapped up, Mavis hurried on. "I think Nana Lucy had a hand in his decision, but he came to me all on his own."

A shiver of fear ran down her back, and she stood and hurried to the fence. Throwing both arms across the top rail, she managed to keep from collapsing.

What the hell had she ever done to deserve this? But she knew. It was her fault she'd lost the baby, and God was finally paying her back.

"Randi, it's the perfect solution."

"Perfect for who. Why would Davie do this?" He was the one who'd hurt her, not the other way around, and not for a moment did she believe he wanted to make up for the pain he'd caused. He might have convinced everyone else he'd grown up, but she knew from personal experience people didn't change.

"Perfect for you. We all know Davie doesn't want to be married any more than you do. He'd want out as soon as the time's up." Mavis moved closer and leaned alongside Randi. "He wants to buy some registered cows, and this is the quickest way to build his herd."

"Sure, he says that now, but after a month or two, he'll decide he's had enough fun and leave me to pick up the mess."

As usual.

A feeling of sadness almost strong enough to drop her to her knees settled onto Randi's shoulders.

"No, he won't. Dex talked to him, and so did Nana."

Randi felt the weight of her friend's arm around her shoulder. "Aren't you ready to tell me what happened? You've been unhappy for a long time now. Let me help."

"Nothing happened." Randi pulled herself together and straightened. She sucked in a deep breath and blew it out. Turning to her friend, she attempted to smile. "This was a fool idea from the start, and I can't believe I've spent so much time worrying about it. Tell Davie thanks, but no thanks."

Mavis smiled in return, but sadness still colored her eyes. "Tell him yourself. He just pulled up your driveway."

Randi whirled just in time to see Davie's new Dodge stop by the side of her house. "You invited him here?"

"He said he wanted to talk to you, but you probably wouldn't let him, so I told him to come down when I was here." Mavis grinned. "You only have until tomorrow. I know you don't like Davie, and I know you have your reasons, but you can't just throw away that much money.

You and Davie can do this."

Randi stared at her so-called friend. The waves of anger and fear radiating off her should have knocked Mavis over. "I have to look through the paperwork again. Do I lose the money if I kill him before the six months are up?" With a sigh, she climbed the rails and perched on the top of the pasture fence. At least this way she could look down on Davie.

He swaggered around the corner of the house, the smile that had gotten her into so much trouble firmly on his handsome face. Stopping a few feet away, he stuffed his hands into the pockets of his jeans. "Is it safe to come closer?"

Randi shrugged.

"I'm almost sure she won't fly off the fence at you, but it might be safer if you stay out of arm's reach." Mavis leaned against the fence and looked up at Randi. "What's your decision?"

Randi's head hurt, and her heart hurt. Since the day her father had died, she'd had a plan for her future—clear-cut and well thought out. When had the plan become a boggy mess?

How was she supposed to make a life-changing decision the way things were now? But, if she didn't make the decision, it would be made for her.

She raised her gaze and glared at Davie. "Why are you doing this?"

The grin fell off his face, and he stayed silent for a long moment. Finally, he walked over to the fence and climbed up beside her. "I need the money."

If he'd tried to convince her he wanted to help, she'd have pushed him off. Money was the only reason she would believe. If he needed cash bad enough, he'd see this farce through to the end. "Okay."

Both Davie and Mavis stared at her.

"I said okay."

Without a word, Davie hopped down from the fence.

As she started to jump, he grasped her around the waist and lifted her gently to the ground.

She whirled away. "Get your hands off me."

Davie stepped back and smiled. "I just thought since we're getting married, I should act like the loving fiancé."

"You don't touch me except when the cameras are rolling. The rest of the time, it's hands off or the deal's off." She stormed to the house, climbed the stairs and slammed the door behind her.

Throwing herself onto the couch, she pulled a throw pillow over her face. If she blocked them both out, maybe they'd leave. She didn't want the damned money anyway.

The sound of the back door opening and then quietly closing echoed through the room. Randi pulled the pillow tighter across her face. "Mavis, this isn't going to work."

"It won't work if you keep up that attitude. You need to work on being more positive."

At the sound of Davie's deep voice, she shot to her feet and the pillow went flying.

Davie reached out and caught it mid-air. He handed it back. His smile widened, and he took a step toward her, his dark eyes following her every move. "I want the money. It's the quickest way to get my own herd, but if you really don't want to do this, I understand."

She looked at the man she'd loved with all her heart. Had he really changed like Mavis said, or was this just another example of Davie grinning his way to what he wanted?

"You don't understand anything."

#

Davie had always been proud of the fact that no matter how many other ways he'd screwed up his life, he'd never been a coward. Sure, he'd wanted to run when Randi told him she was pregnant, but he hadn't. He hadn't left until after she'd told him there wasn't a baby.

That wasn't true anymore.

After almost fifteen minutes of sitting in his pickup, too nervous to go into the hotel where he was supposed to meet Randi and the *Your Dream Wedding* coordinator, he still hadn't gotten the nerve to finalize the agreement with the show.

What had he gotten himself into? When he'd been younger, he'd been known for making snap decisions and having to live with the consequences. He'd thought he'd changed his ways a few years ago.

Apparently not.

Being engaged to Randi for several months and married to her for half a year was going to be one of the hardest things he'd ever done. He wasn't sure he could be around her day after day and keep his hands off.

He was certain she'd kill him if he couldn't.

The payoff would get him to his goals much faster, but that wasn't the real reason he'd agreed to become Randi's bridegroom. He knew she needed cash, and this was the only way she'd ever take a dime from him.

The big carved wooden door opened, and Randi stuck her head out, a scowl on her face.

The time for wasting time was done. Davie climbed out of his truck and strode toward Randi, a smile pasted on his face. "Are we ready?"

Her frown deepened. "We've been ready." She waved her hand in a circle indicating everyone but him. "We've been waiting for a half hour for you to show up."

He slung his arm around her shoulder and pulled her to him. "I'm not that late. I just got hung up in traffic. If you'd have let me ride in with you, we wouldn't have a problem."

She raised her gaze to meet his eyes, her voice barely above a whisper. "I thought you weren't coming."

The desolate look on her face made his stomach clench. While he'd been worrying about his own problems, he'd caused her more stress. "Look, I'm sorry. I was nervous about doing all this."

She shrugged and moved a few steps away, before looking at him again. "You want to back out? Now's the time."

Davie hadn't been close to her for six years, but her scent wafted across his nerve endings like it had been yesterday. "I don't want to back out."

She gave him a quick nod and hurried inside.

A tall man with a high forehead and shoulder length hair pulled into a thin ponytail nearly ran down the hall as they entered the building. His dark suit must have been custom made. At six feet two inches, Davie had to look a long ways up to see the guys face. "Is everything all right?"

Randi moved a little closer, her sigh so powerful it could have moved a forty-foot sailboat. "Davie, this is Eldon Hughes, one of the producers of *Your Dream Wedding*. Mr. Hughes, this is my um—he's my ..."

A smile took some of the starkness from Hughes' face. "This must be the wonderful man you're going to marry."

With another gigantic sigh, Randi turned on her heel and left Davie standing with Vincent Schiavelli's nerdy brother. Without another choice, Davie held out his hand to the man. "Nice to meet you."

Hughes ignored the hand and pulled him into a hug. "I'm so excited to meet Randi's future husband.

Future husband? There had been numerous discussions about the wedding with their family and friends, but him being a husband hadn't been mentioned and the word blew him away. He was going to be a husband. "I need to find Randi."

As the man spoke again, Davie strained to hear the softly spoken words. "Of course. Follow me. She's probably looking at the photos of our exquisite wedding dresses and trying to choose."

"Probably." But probably not. Davie followed the man down the hall and when they reached a set of double doors, Hughes stopped.

"I'm going to get us something to drink. Just make yourself comfortable in here, and I'll be back in a moment."

As Hughes hurried on down the hall, Davie took a deep breath and entered the room. A group of five folding chairs had been set up around a circular table. The white lace tablecloth was topped with a large bouquet of red roses and several lace-covered three ring binders.

Randi sat in one of the chairs, her head in her hands, the picture of dejection. More than anything, Davie wanted to take her in his arms and reassure her that everything would be all right, but he couldn't. He wasn't sure it would, and he'd vowed to never lie to Randi again.

He moved back outside the door and raised his voice. "Thanks, Mr. Hughes. Randi and I would both like a Coke." He made a little extra noise as he reentered the room.

Randi stood beside the table, flipping through one of the books. When she looked up, there was a trace of redness around her eyes. "Where's Hughes?"

"He thought we could use something to drink. I suggested whiskey, but he didn't think that was wise. I ordered us Cokes, mine regular and I told him to get a diet for you."

The red around her eyes was overshadowed by the angry flush covering her cheeks. "I don't drink diet. Maybe you could ask about my preferences if you don't know what I like."

He'd been smiling at her self-righteous anger, but the grin faded as he thought about her words from before. "If we're going to make this work, you might practice calling me your fiancé, and try not to look physically sick when you talk about the wedding."

"You're right." As they heard footsteps coming down the hall, Randi's smile transformed her expression. She moved close to him and put her arm through his. The kiss she gave him as Hughes entered the room stopped him in his tracks.

Oh, how he remembered her kisses, and he'd never found another woman who turned him on like Randi.

"I always like to see lovebirds. Not everyone who wins this wedding package is in love, you know." Hughes put the small tray he was carrying on the table and filled three glasses with water before turning to them and indicating the chairs. "Won't you have a seat? And before I forget. One of our other couples pulled out and we'd like for you to fill in the spot."

"What does that mean?" Randi's natural suspicions were on high alert.

"We'll perform the wedding ceremony in about a month from today."

Shock rendered him speechless for a moment, as it must have Randi. He didn't hear a word coming from her. "One month? I don't know anything about weddings, but they take longer than that to set up, right?"

"We've done hundreds of weddings. This is a piece of wedding cake for us. Pardon the pun." Hughes grinned and pushed a stack of papers toward each of them.

"What happened to the other couple?" Randi made no effort to look at the papers. "Did they call off the wedding?"

"No, we found out they were already married. That's strictly against the terms of this contract." Hughes pointed to the stack of papers.

"People try to fake this?" Randi's voice had a small quiver in it as she spoke.

At the sight of a blush spreading across her cheeks, Davie gave her hand a squeeze.

"There are some people who are unethical. They want the money and the honeymoon. Let's sit down, shall we?" Mr. Hughes took his glass and chose a seat.

"What happens when you catch them?" Davie pulled out Randi's chair and waited for her to sit before scooting his closer to hers.

Randi started to frown then managed a passible smile. "I can't imagine."

"We file fraud charges and throw them in jail."

Davie's heart pushed his blood through his veins at a frantic pace. He was just trying to help Randi, to make up for his actions, but he didn't want to go to jail or lose the ranch in some kind of settlement. He moved closer to her and put his arm around her shoulder.

Hughes laughed. "Not really. No one gets the money until they've completed the six months of marriage. And, our contract is iron clad. If we find out they are trying to pull one over on us, we air the footage we have and let everyone know." He opened his briefcase and pulled out a stack of folders, handing one to each of them.

"If one half of the couple pulls out, the other one gets all the money and we air the break-up." His grin told Davie he didn't care which way things went. At least they wouldn't go to jail, but having the show tell the world he was a crook wasn't his first choice for a way to become famous.

Davie opened the file and began reading the top page. Legalese. He'd have to get the ranch's attorney to look this over before he signed. But one thing jumped out at him. "What's this about you filming us before the wedding?" He scooted closer to Randi and laid his hand on her thigh.

"Oh, yes. That's the most fun part. Normally, we'd set up several games or contests and film you and Randi playing them. Since we're so short of time, you'll only have to do one."

The frown on Randi's face made her almost unrecognizable.

The toughest woman he knew was worried. He could see it in her eyes. Without thinking, he leaned across and gave her a kiss.

CHAPTER FOUR

After nearly a week of heart pounding panic after the meeting with the television producer, Randi had finally broken down and asked Mavis to meet her.

The scent of freshly ground coffee and baked goods filled the air as Randi opened the door to the Shamrock. Hurrying to the back of the room, she slid into the booth across from her friend.

Before she could open her mouth, Gladys hurried up with a cup and a pot of coffee. "Here you go, sweetie. I was so sorry to hear about your horse. Such a terrible thing to happen. Now, what do you want to eat?"

Randi took a long swallow for the coffee, enjoying the sting of the hot liquid as it melted the lump in her throat. She shook her head, blinking away tears. "Nothing right now, Gladys. Maybe in a few minutes." Her throat was so tight with worry she couldn't even swallow a bite of Clarence's world-class pie.

Gladys nodded and hurried away.

Mavis took the silver pitcher of cream and poured a generous amount into her mug. She expertly stacked four packets of sugar, tore off the tops in one quick move and stirred the sweetener into the steaming liquid. "I can't seem to make coffee like Gladys does. Why is that?"

"Because you can't cook anything." Randi took another swallow of the black coffee before adding a healthy dose of both cream and sugar. She normally took hers black, but all the worry was causing her stomach to do back flips. "We met with the show's representatives last week and signed the papers."

"And?"

Her normally talkative friend was getting on her nerves, but when your nerves are frayed to the point of breaking, anything gets on them. "And, he said some people try to defraud the show. I about jumped out of my skin. It's a good thing Davie is level-headed." She stopped and looked at Mavis, her eyes wide. "I can't believe I said that."

A smile spread across Mavis' face. "Doesn't sound like you for sure."

Randi managed a small grin. "I nearly ran out of the meeting, but Davie kept asking questions."

Mavis lowered her voice and leaned across the table. "What happens if they find out you and Davie aren't in love? You couldn't get thrown in jail, could you? Because, I think you'd come out okay, but Davie in jail . . ."

Randi shook her head. Mavis thought she was a lot tougher than she was. "We don't get paid until the wedding is done and the six months are up. If we don't follow through, no money would change hands, but it's in the contract that they own all the footage, and they air it along with our names. He smiled when he told us they find the most embarrassing shots to air."

"Well, at least there isn't jail time."

"I'm not sure jail wouldn't be the better option. Can you imagine living in this town with everyone having watched the show?" The rhythm of Randi's heart had just become normal, but the thought of the teasing she and Davie would endure had it racing again. "I'd have to move."

"Well, we won't let that happen. Your sisters, Dex and

I are the only people on the face of the earth who know the real reason you and Davie are getting married, and we're not telling. If you can keep from killing your fiancé before the wedding, you've got it made."

"And Nana Lucy. She'd take great delight in seeing me crash and burn."

"But if you did, so would Davie. Nana wouldn't let that happen."

"No, she wouldn't." The woman loved her grandsons and would protect them with her life.

How in the hell had she allowed herself to get maneuvered into this mess? Mavis was right about one thing, though. If they could pretend they liked each other, maybe they could pull off the wedding.

Probably.

She thought of the Davie she'd known before.

Better make that, possibly.

"It looks like you're feeling better. Your face has some color, at least. You looked like Casper the Friendly Ghost when you walked in." Mavis took another sip of her coffee and waved at Gladys. "Is there any of Clarence's pie left?"

"Today's been a slow day," Gladys said as she wiped up a few drips of coffee Randi had spilled. "What kind do you want?"

Mavis grinned. "Surprise us."

As Gladys hurried away, Mavis looked at Randi. "Now that I've fixed the problem, do you have any others?"

Randi waited as Gladys set a plate in front of each of them. Red, rich cherries peeked out from beneath a flaky crust. She'd never tasted better pie anywhere.

"Ahhh," Mavis groaned. "I never thought I'd like Pecan Pie. Who ever thought of making pies out of nuts? But, Clarence is a wizard." She looked up, her mouth full. After swallowing, she grinned. "What's next on the list?"

Randi stared into her half-eaten cherry pie. No way could she make eye contact and say what she had to say.

"Well, spit it out."

"I know it's late to ask you this, but I was hoping if I waited long enough I could figure a way out." Randi raised the fork to her mouth then put it back on the plate. No way could she swallow. "I'm supposed to go pick out my wedding dress."

Mavis did a fist pump. "When? This weekend? Can I go, too?"

Gladys looked up from the crossword puzzle she was working.

If Mavis were closer, Randi would have slapped her hand over her friend's mouth. "Shhh! Do you want everyone to find out?" She gave Mavis the stink-eye until she quieted. "I'm counting on you coming to pick one out for me. There's only one problem."

Mavis raised an eyebrow and waited.

What a classic look. Randi had never been able to raise just one eyebrow. Never one to be a quitter, she tried again.

"Do you have something in your eye?" Mavis tried and failed to keep a straight face.

"No, I don't. The problem is the fitting is today. In about an hour in Boise, so we'd have to leave now."

Mavis pulled out her phone and glanced at the time. "We can make it. Let me call Dex and tell him I'm not going to be home for a while."

In moments, they were one the highway to Boise. With fifteen minutes to spare, they pulled into the hotel where Randi and Davie had met Mr. Hughes just a week before.

The women found a room filled with racks of frilly white wedding dresses. Randi contemplated running for the truck, but Mavis had a death grip on her arm.

A blonde with a curly up-do hurried across the room. The woman was scary thin and wore more make-up than Randi had at any time in her life, including Halloween. "Miss Bachmann, I'm Giselle. So good to see you. Are you ready to find your dream dress?"

Randi almost let her true feelings, along with her panic

out, but this wasn't Giselle's fault. "Sure. Find me a great one."

The young woman ran her hands along a line of dresses and pulled out one, displaying it over her arm. She glided toward Randi and held out the voluminous white costume. "What do you think of this one?"

"I'd look like a Disney princess on steroids. I'll pass." Randi sank into the pretty pink silk chair and put her head in her hands. "Can I go home now?"

"No," Mavis said and began rummaging through the racks.

Three hours and twelve dresses later, Randi was no nearer to finding something she could stand than she'd been when they walked in the door. Everything they'd shown her had been too poufy, too sparkly, or way too elaborate for a cowgirl. And they were all so white.

Her braid had come undone around the tenth dress, and her hair hung loosely around her shoulders. "Damn it all anyway." She stuffed her fingers through the locks and attempted to re-do her braid.

"Could you excuse us for a moment?" Mavis asked Giselle. "We need to talk."

As soon as the door closed behind Claire, Mavis rounded on Randi. "I know this isn't your idea of fun, but you decided to do this, for a very good reason I might add, and you'd better quit complaining. It's only going to take six months, and you'll be able to make your biggest dream come true. How many people get an opportunity like this?"

Damn it!

Mavis was right, and she'd been acting like a spoiled child. Randi stood and straightened. "Bring Claire back in here and let's find a dress."

#

Davie hadn't seen Randi for a week, and he was getting

a little twitchy. The desire to be near her, the desire he'd held at bay for six years, was growing stronger with each passing hour. He'd never had a problem boxing up his emotions and storing them away from his day-to-day life.

Since he'd returned to the Rafter D, his filing system had exploded. The last few days he'd driven by her house and considered stopping to chat.

Not that she'd chat. She'd probably throw something at him.

Their meeting today with the caterer couldn't have come at a better time. He'd get to spend an hour or so with Randi, and she couldn't walk away or even scream at him.

He hoped.

After parking behind the storefront in downtown Boise, he hurried in the rear entrance.

Randi grabbed his arm as he entered the business and pulled him off to the side. "Where have you been?" Her voice was an angry whisper. "I've been waiting fifteen minutes, and these people are forcing me to taste things that are just nasty. Although I guess if the food's bad, we don't have to buy as much."

"We're not buying any of it, the show is." Taking his life in his hands, he threw his arm around her shoulders. "Come on." He'd never considered food to be feminine or masculine, but with the interior walls the palest pink, he was re-evaluating. The round table at the back of the shop was covered with a royal purple tablecloth topped with lace. A huge gold and crystal chandelier hung over the table. Femininity oozed from this place.

Even Randi looked as out of place as a wolverine in a—. He didn't want to finish that thought.

A young woman in a royal blue micro-mini dress and sky-high crimson heels hurried toward them, a smile on her face. "We were so excited when the people from *Your Dream Wedding* called to say we'd been chosen to cater your nuptials. Elegance Catering will do everything in our power to make your wedding a dream come true." She turned to smile at Davie. "Your fiancé wanted to wait for you to arrive, so if you'll both have a seat, I'll bring out a selection of our favorites."

Davie scooted his chair so close to Randi that their legs touched. Her scathing look made him laugh. "What?"

Before she could get off a shot, the young woman brought a tray filled with various plates of something.

A lot of somethings he'd never seen before.

"First, let me introduce myself. I'm Sheila. I'll be your epicurean connoisseur."

Davie's brows drew together. When he looked at Randi, she shrugged.

Sheila forced a smile then waved her arm at the food as if she was a game show host. "We've put together a tasting of delicacies from around the world."

Randi leaned away from the table, and it was all Davie could do to not join her. She pointed to one plate. "What the heck is that?"

The caterer's voice took on a note of strain. "I've served you Temaki with salmon, radish sprouts, Tobiko, cucumber, and Ikura." Her smile wavered.

"That looks like the fish eggs my daddy used to catch trout when we were little." Randi turned to Davie and grinned. "Remember when you fell in the river trying to catch that frog?"

The caterer stopped her eye roll mid-roll and widened the stiff smile on her face. "That is very expensive salmon roe."

Davie knew he'd better step in before Randi told the woman what she really thought. "I don't think sushi's exactly right for what we've got in mind. Can you show us something else?"

"Let's pick out the appetizers later. I've got really special dishes for the main course." Her smile warmed as she looked at Davie and placed another plate in front of him.

The piece of rare beef looked fantastic, but it was so small he could have eaten it in two bites. What he thought might be potatoes were the size of marbles. One green bean and one tiny ear of corn lay across the top of the meat with a gob of something that looked like catsup on top.

He glanced up at her expecting her to laugh at the joke she'd pulled, but she simply seemed to be waiting for him to taste the fancy fare. "Um. This is a sample, right?"

"Each of your guests will receive a plate just like this. The Kobe beef is aged for eighty days and is to die for."

He glanced at Randi to see her leaning back in her chair, her arms crossed, a smile on her face. No help there.

Davie cut off a bite and offered it to Randi. As she chewed, her eyes closed and she moaned. He took what was left and popped it into his mouth.

He would have chewed if the meat hadn't melted in his mouth. "This is good, really good, but I just don't think this will be enough for our guests. Can you put twice as much on the plate? And maybe some mashed potatoes and gravy or a baked potato? My grandmother could make some dinner rolls."

Randi laughed, and Davie closed his eyes to savor the sound. There'd been a time when she'd laughed at everything, but he hadn't heard it for years. Maybe she did still laugh, just not around him.

Sheila pulled out a chair and plopped down. Her sigh was big enough to have blown the beef off the plate if they hadn't eaten it all. "The contract we signed with *Your Dream Wedding* stipulated a per plate maximum. This dish has the budget maxed out." The young woman picked up a plate filled with what looked like chicken fried steaks, one of Davie's favorites. "Try this. I can give your guests a much bigger serving."

Expecting beef, Davie was surprised when the inside was white. "What is this?"

Randi laughed again. "This isn't going to work." She

looked at the woman, a wide smile on her face. "Davie's family raises beef, and so do most of our guests. I don't think they'll be happy with tofu no matter how good it is."

Sheila tapped her front tooth with her gold and purple pen. "I have an idea." She pushed the plate aside and slid a three-tiered serving dish between the two of them. "This is our selection of desserts. Help yourselves while I make a phone call."

Sheila hurried away as Davie eyed the array of sweets. Thank goodness they had fancy paper labels. "Crepes Suzette, Norman Tart, Mocha Pots de Crème, and, Profiterole" The names were all hand-printed on cream parchment in a beautiful flowing script. He laid his hand on Randi's thigh and grinned. "Looks more like skinny pancakes, apple pie, chocolate pudding and cream-filled donuts with chocolate frosting."

She put her hand on his, picked up a Profiterole and held it to his lips. "Try a donut."

The flaky pastry melted in his mouth. The chocolate glaze enhanced the flavor of the vanilla cream filling. As he chewed, Davie watched Randi take a bite of the Mocha Crème.

"Mmmm, chocolate." Without thinking, he leaned closer and kissed her. To his surprise, she kissed him back. She didn't fall into his arms, but she didn't pull away either. That was progress.

He was on the verge of suggesting they take the kiss back home, when Sheila came hurrying in from the back room of the store.

She was slightly flushed, and she had a genuine smile on her face. "I think I've solved our problem. My little brother owns Three Rivers Barbeque. You'll think you've died and gone to heaven when you sink your teeth into something he's cooked. What would you think about BBQ ribs, marinated brisket, and spiced pork tenderloin?" She rocked back on her impossibly high heels and grinned.

"Will *Your Dream Wedding* go along with this?" Davie

looked from Randi to Sheila and back.

"Who cares?" Randi said. "I'll pay for it myself if they don't. I've heard about your brother and his magic barbeque. When can we talk to him?"

Sheila held out a small scrap of paper. "Here's his phone number. I told him you'd be calling."

"We'd like some of every dessert you brought out." Davie looked at Randi. "Is that okay with you?"

"That's perfect." Randi slipped her arm through Davie's. "If nothing else, no one is going home hungry from our wedding."

CHAPTER FIVE

Pulling into a turnout on the hill above Jordan Valley, Randi cut the engine of her truck. She climbed out and walked to the edge of the asphalt. Looking out over the green land around Succor Creek, she procrastinated. The more time she spent here, the less time she'd have to be sociable at the party at the Dunbar Ranch.

She wasn't hospitable on her best day, and stress was chasing away what little ability for small talk she possessed. It was just her luck to be marrying a cowboy with an overabundance of friends and family.

Luck had been a sparse commodity for most of her life. Her dad died when she'd been thirteen, and her mother had left the day Camille turned eighteen.

She'd gotten by because she'd had her sisters, along with Mavis, and most of all, Davie. But when Davie had left her six years ago, any luck she'd acquired had vanished.

She wrapped her arms around her waist and took several deep breaths. This wasn't Davie's fault. Sure he'd run out on her, but then she hadn't told him the whole truth either.

She'd wanted him to pick her without reservation. She'd wanted him to love her more than his freedom.

She'd wanted him to show more maturity than either of them were capable of at the time.

Maybe it was time to stop blaming Davie for all her problems.

The beep of a text coming in broke into her thoughts. Mavis was wondering why she hadn't made it to the ranch yet. She stuffed the phone back in her pocket.

As she took a few steps toward the truck, the toe of her boot caught on something.

A dull silver object peeked out of the gravel. It was a Jordan Valley High School ring. The red stone gleamed dully in the afternoon sunshine, and when he turned it over, she realized it was from the year Davie graduated.

It wasn't Davie's though. His was tucked in the back of her underwear drawer and hadn't seen the light of day or the dark of night for six years. She'd taken it off the day she'd learned Davie had left the area, had left her alone to cope with an unplanned pregnancy. But for some reason, she hadn't been able to throw it away, or even give it back to his family.

Foolish hope seemed have woven tendrils into her mind.

Randi tucked the ring into her pocket and climbed into the truck. The ranch was only a few miles down the road, and before Mavis could text her again, she'd pulled into the driveway.

The yard was full of people. Neighbors and friends who wanted to congratulate and tease the newly engaged couple gathered around her before she'd even gotten out of her truck.

"Can I see your ring?" Tilly Thompson's high-pitched voice carried across the crowd. Silence fell over the guests, and they crowded closer to Randi.

"I—we haven't picked one out yet." She forced a laugh. "We haven't had time."

Old man Bellows yelled from the front porch. "Thought you didn't like Davie."

Randi steeled herself for more embarrassing questions. For the sake of the money, and to avoid embarrassing Davie, she had to make this look real.

Before she could say anything, Davie appeared by her side. He took her hand and led her to the porch before turning to all their friends. "I have two announcements. First, Drew called, and Chelsey has offered to sing at the wedding and do a private concert during the reception."

A cheer went up from the crowd. It wasn't every day a country artist voted best new voice at the CMA Awards did a performance in this small town.

"Now for the most important thing." Davie dropped to one knee, and Randi felt heat crawl up her cheeks. He held a small blue box in front of her and opened the top.

A halo of smaller stones surrounded a large round diamond creating a floral effect. Dazzling diamond accents adorned the platinum band. The ring was stunning as it glittered in the sun. It was everything an engagement ring should be, and she hated it.

She stood frozen in place as Davie took her hand. "Miranda Bachmann, will you marry me?"

The silence was so thick she thought she could hear a snake work its way through the tall grass surrounding the porch. She almost hoped it was a rattler because the commotion would get her out of this awkward situation.

There was no way she could feed or clean stalls in that glamorous ring. She wouldn't dare rope for fear of losing the center stone. It was totally impractical. It was totally not her. Randi looked at Davie. She half expected him to have that smart-ass look on his face, happy that he'd blown her away with this.

Instead, he stared at her with such uncertainty she forced her mouth shut so she wouldn't say what she'd been thinking.

Fixing her gaze on Davie, she nodded. When he didn't move, she cleared her throat. "Yes, I'll marry you, but don't think that means I'll do all the cooking." She managed a cocky grin. Keeping their conversations filled with sarcasm was the only way she was going to get through this.

He didn't grin back. It was almost as if she'd hurt his feelings, but that couldn't be right. Wild child Davie Dunbar couldn't be serious about the wedding. They were both in this for the money no matter how much she wished it were real.

He had to be playing the part.

Davie stood and pulled her into his arms. When his lips touched hers, she forgot for a moment that this was play-acting. She melted into his arms, but the knowledge that if he just hadn't left all those years ago, they could have this for real nearly did her in.

To the hoots and cheers of the crowd, she pulled back and looked in Davie's eyes. She was on the verge of diving back in for another kiss when Davie's grandmother tapped her on the arm.

"Congratulations, Randi."

Randi gave her a short hug. "Thanks, Lucy."

"I just want you to promise me one thing. You take good care of this boy. We Dunbars marry for life, you know."

And what did she say to that? She looked to Davie for help, and he wrapped an arm around his grandmother. "Now Nana. I'll be the one taking care of her. You don't need to worry."

Before Lucy could say another word, Randi and Davie were surrounded by a group of young women. Everyone wanted to see the ring, and reluctantly, Randi held out her hand. Davie excused himself, and Randi watched as he joined Dex and Rafe.

"This is so beautiful." Julie Latah sighed wistfully. She held out her hand next to Randi's, her stone tiny against the size of Randi's diamond. "Mine's not as big, but Roy spent every last dime he had, and I love it."

And there it was again. The difference between getting

married for love and getting married for money. She managed a smile for Julie. "Yours is very pretty. I can see Roy's love shining through."

Julie gave her a hug and hurried over to her new husband.

"Didn't take you long to get your hooks into a Dunbar." The venomous whisper caught her by surprise. Randi whirled to see Dena standing behind her.

The thin woman hair was scraped back into a ponytail and she wore too big jeans and a threadbare T-shirt. The sneer on her face almost caused Randi to run for cover. "Mavis tricked Dex into marriage and now you. These people must be blind. It's obvious you don't love Davie."

It was that obvious? She'd worked hard not to let her true feelings show. At a loss as to what to say to Dena, she scanned the crowd, looking for a friendly face. As their eyes met, Nana Lucy gave Randi a tight smile.

It wasn't exactly the face she'd been looking for, and it was pretty obvious Davie's grandmother wasn't happy about the pending nuptials, but anyone was better than Dena.

"Don't depend on Lucy to welcome you into the family." The hatred in Dena's expression caused Randi to take a step back before she caught herself. "She and I seem to be the only ones who see you for the gold-digger you really are."

Randi's first reaction was to put Dena in her place, but this was her betrothal party and getting into a hair-pulling contest with a woman who used to be her friend probably wouldn't do anybody any good. Besides, since Dena's dad had died, she was the unhappiest person Randi had ever seen. No use adding to the woman's misery.

Randi turned away to find Nana Lucy standing behind her.

The small woman took Randi's hand in hers and headed for the kitchen. "Mavis, come with us." It wasn't a request.

When they were in the house, Nana Lucy shut and locked the door. She stood on her tiptoes to get eye to eye with Randi. "I don't know what you two are up to, but it's not good. If you hurt my Davie, I'll come after you personally."

Randi was frozen in place. She wasn't scared, not really. Nana Lucy was in good shape for eighty, but she was still almost sixty years Randi's senior. The shock came because she'd always gotten along with Davie's grandmother. She'd spilled her heart to Lucy more than once during her high school years.

Mavis moved between them. "Lucy, this is between Randi and Davie. They're both adults, and they can make their own decisions."

Lucy poured three glasses of iced tea and placed them on the table before sitting down.

Randi would have preferred to go back out with the crowd, but she didn't have much choice at this point. She sat and took a long pull on the tea.

Lucy stared at her. She took a drink and set the glass on the table. "Can you tell me you love my grandson?"

"Of course she can," Mavis said.

The look Lucy gave her granddaughter-in-law made Mavis shut her mouth. Shifting her gaze to Randi, she continued. "Davie has pined over you for years. If you can't promise me you love him with all your heart, you're going to break his."

Randi stood and walked to the window. Without thinking, she held out her left hand, tilting it back and forth while she stared at the beautiful ring Davie had given her. He couldn't have surprised her more, and she wished she felt something other than sadness. She had loved him with all her heart, and maybe still did, but it didn't make any difference. She wasn't ready to risk her heart on him again.

Lucy cleared her throat, but Randi didn't turn around. Scores of people were out there having a good time with

Davie at the center of the festivities, and she was in here being grilled. This was supposed to be so easy. Get married, live side by side for six months, collect the money and go on with their lives.

She turned slowly and let her gaze roam around the familiar room. Although Mavis had helped paint the living room and bathroom, they hadn't gotten around to changing the kitchen. Lucy and Davie's mom had put up the wallpaper the year before his mother had died in an accident.

This had been a safe, warm place for Randi as long as she could remember. She sat beside Lucy and took her hand. "I can tell you we both know what we're doing. We've talked this through, and we have a plan." She reached out and gave Lucy a hug. "I can promise I won't intentionally hurt him." A movement by the arch leading to the living room caught Randi's attention.

Davie stood just outside the room, listening. Served him right. She'd thought of telling Lucy what she wanted to hear, that Randi loved Davie. She'd opened her mouth to do just that, but the words hadn't come out.

She said the only other thing she could think of—the truth.

#

Davie pulled up in front of Randi's house and killed the engine. Before Randi had left, he'd convinced her to meet with him in the morning. They needed to get their stories straight for their meeting with the representative from *Your Dream Wedding* in this afternoon.

And he'd brought a bribe.

The door to the small house opened, and Randi stepped out onto the porch. Shadows hid her face, but she was barefoot, dressed in ragged cut-off jeans and a Cruel Girl tank top. Moving to the edge of the porch, she shaded her eyes as she watched him climb out of his Dodge.

He pulled his gaze from her and let it wander around the property. The fences were in good shape, but the house was on the verge of falling down. Leave it to Randi to make sure her horses were safe, but not worry about her home. She'd always been the champion of the underdog.

He walked around the truck and opened the passenger door. As he opened the cat carrier, a muffled whine filled the cab. A fuzzy red and white pup climbed his shirt to curl below his chin. He was playing to Randi's soft side.

As he climbed the rickety wooden steps, he held out the squirming ball of fluff. "I brought you an engagement present. Her name is Tripper." The pup squirmed as Randi lifted the animal from his hands.

"This is the best fake engagement present you could have picked." She cuddled the puppy beneath her chin and laughed as it licked her neck. When she raised her gaze to his, they glistened with unshed tears. "My Bruiser died last winter. His heart gave out."

"I know. Dex told me. That was one good old dog." Davie lifted his hand to stroke her hair, but thought better of it. "Going to invite your fiancé in?"

"Fake fiancé, and come on in." She stood back and after he entered, she closed the door and put the pup on the floor. "Where did you get her?"

The puppy scurried around the room, checking out the new environment. When she got close to old dog bed in the corner, the scruff stood up on the back of her neck. High-pitched puppy barks filled the room.

"It was Bruiser's. I couldn't seem to throw it away." Randi dropped to the floor beside Tripper and stroked her head. "This is yours now, pretty girl."

That must have been all the reassurance she needed, because Tripper curled into a ball on the bed and went to sleep.

"Looks like it'll be put to good use," Davie said. "I got her from the Circle J. She's out of one of their best red Aussies."

"Thank you." Randi's voice didn't have a trace of sarcasm, anger, or hatred. A wistful smile brightened her face as she watched the pup sleep. "Her name is Tripper?"

"You can change it if you want. I've had her three days, and I've tripped over her every time I've tried to walk across the room. She's definitely a people puppy." Davie sank on the ancient, green Naugahyde couch and leaned back. He relaxed against the cracked fabric and closed his eyes.

Randi had left the party early, pleading a headache, and Davie had spent the rest of the evening fending off well-meaning friends and relatives who wanted to know when he'd popped the question and how soon the wedding was going to be.

Something icy touched the back of his hand and his eyes flew open. "Whaaa!" At the sound of Randi's giggle, he focused on her face. He loved both the laugh and the happy expression. He loved everything about her.

She held a glass filled with ice and cola. "Sorry to wake you. I thought you might like a Coke, but maybe I should have let you sleep. Party too much last night?"

"If you can call trying to convince all our friends and neighbors that the company who does this as a business doesn't need their advice on planning a wedding, then yes. Dex and Rafe egged them on until I had to sic Nana Lucy on them."

"Did any of them have good ideas?" Randi sat beside him and sipped her drink.

"Johnny Juker wants to play his ukulele at the reception, Martha Campbell offered to make those awful cupcakes she takes to every fundraiser, and Dex said we could get married in their front yard, overlooking the canyon. I bet Mr. Hughes would love that." Davie leaned closer and bumped Randi's shoulder with his. "Can you see his face at the thought of an outdoor wedding among the sagebrush and Junipers?"

"He definitely won't like the grasshoppers." Randi sat

up and bumped Davie back. "Wait! We haven't settled on a venue yet. I like the idea of using the ranch." The smile on her face faded away, and her brows drew down in a frown. "Unless you don't want to. I mean, you'll probably get married for real one of these days and that's a lovely place to have a wedding."

"I think us getting married at the ranch is a great idea." He couldn't imagine marrying another woman. As far as he was concerned, this was his one and only wedding. Now if he could convince Randi.

"We'll need to convince Mr. Hughes that the viewers will love a ranch setting. Market share seems to be his deciding factor." She walked into the kitchen and put her glass in the sink. "It's about time to leave. Give me a few minutes to figure out a place to put Tripper while we're gone."

"I brought a small kennel that will work until she grows out of it. By that time, I'll have something else built." Davie reached down and stroked the puppy's head.

Tripper groaned and rolled to her side, stretching out her stubby legs before going back to sleep.

Randi stood in the kitchen doorway watching him. "You don't need to trouble yourself. I can figure out something."

"It's no trouble. There's a chain link dog run in the old barn. I'll bring it down when you're ready." He stood and walked over to Randi. "I forgot to bring her veterinary records. She's had all her shots and been wormed."

"Thanks, Davie. I'll change my clothes and be ready in a minute." Without another word, Randi headed down the hallway to the bedroom.

While he waited, Davie walked into the kitchen to put his glass away. The old cabinets had a bright white coat of paint and now, the walls were pale yellow. Both were so recent he could smell the paint. Randi had been busy.

Years ago, when they'd been dating, she'd loved to talk about how she would decorate their house when they got married. If he hadn't been such a coward, they might be married now. Footsteps coming down the hall brought him out of his reverie.

Randi was dressed in pressed jeans, a dark turquoise T-shirt and cowboy boots. She couldn't have looked more beautiful if she'd been in an expensive dinner gown. She grabbed her small, tooled leather backpack and grinned. "I'm ready."

"If I hadn't left, do you think we'd be together today?" He was as shocked by the words that had come out of his mouth as she looked. He'd been thinking about their relationship years ago but hadn't intended to say anything. Sometimes his mouth ran off without consulting his brain. "Never mind." He started toward the door.

Randi stuck out her arm and stopped him. "I guess we'll never know because you didn't stay around to find out." Her hand rested on his upper arm, and her gaze shifted to where she was touching him.

He reached over and covered her hand, holding it against his skin. "I'm sorry. I've made a lot of mistakes in my life, but leaving you is the one thing I truly regret."

STEPHANIE BERGET

CHAPTER SIX

To reward herself for navigating the dual landmines of Davie and Mr. Hughes yesterday, Randi had scheduled a little one on one time with her favorite masseuse. The woman's magic fingers had done her outlook on life a world of good.

As she waited for the light to change, Randi studied at her engagement ring again. It seemed like she'd spent half of her time gazing at the damned, sparkly thing. It really was pretty in a city girl kind of way.

Her thoughts wandered from the ring to events of the day before.

At a loss for words at Davie's apology, she'd almost run to the truck. She'd chattered all the way to Boise to keep Davie from bringing up their past again. By the time they'd reached the hotel where the show was headquartered, she'd been exhausted and unsure what they would do when Hughes refused to use the ranch for the wedding.

But, like many things in her life the last few years, she'd misjudged Mr. Hughes' reaction.

He'd been delighted with the idea of—in his words—a Root'n Toot'n wedding. Their biggest problem had been getting him to release control of the decorations to Mavis and Lucy. He'd wanted to use Holstein colored tablecloths, and provide all the guests with hokey straw hats and plastic bubble pistols. Again, in his words—to make it like a marriage from the Wild, Wild West.

An irritable honk from the car behind her brought her back to the present, and she shifted into gear and hit the gas. Leaving downtown Caldwell behind, she drove through wheat fields and pastures toward Homedale.

Ever since she could remember, the wide-open spaces and soothing green of the farm fields had given Randi a sense of peace. She'd traveled to a lot of places when she'd rodeoed in college, but she'd never lived anywhere but this area. She'd never wanted to . . .

Except for one time. When Davie had left her behind, and she'd faced an unexpected pregnancy alone, she'd wanted to run as far and as fast as she could. The need to live somewhere else disappeared the day she'd been bucked off, but no one, not even Mavis, knew she'd caused her baby's death.

As far as she was concerned, they never would.

Pulling up to the four-way stop in downtown Homedale, she paused for a farm truck to rattle past. As she waited, her mind wandered back to Davie's question. At one time, she'd thought they'd be together forever, but it had only taken the word *pregnant* to make Davie run like a scalded cat.

Now, forever wasn't in her vocabulary.

The drive to her house took just minutes. As she turned into her driveway, she saw Davie's shiny, new truck parked alongside her ramshackle house.

Hell!

How was she supposed to ice down her warming feelings when he was so close she could smell his unique, tempting scent? Pine and dust, cattle and sex. Maybe she couldn't smell the last one, but his scent always brought thoughts of sex to her mind.

At least when she hadn't seen him for years on end, it hadn't been quite so hard to forget he didn't love her enough to stay. She grabbed her backpack and climbed out of the truck.

Stopping for a moment, she allowed herself to drink in the sight of him as he sat on the front porch with the puppy.

Tripper took one quick glance at Randi then growled as she pounced on the large feather Davie held.

"Good to know I don't have to be worried about a turkey feather attacking me with her around." At the sound of Randi's voice, Tripper bounded over and grabbed her pant leg.

Davie picked up a soggy rag. "Or a worn out T-shirt."

She lifted the pup and cradled it in her arms. Starting at its nose, she stroked her fingers over its head and down its back. "You're better than a home alarm system and a whole lot cheaper."

"I'm not sure about the cheaper part." Davie dropped a shoe onto the porch. The toe had suspicious chew marks. "If I was you, I'd keep that nice backpack out of Tripper's reach."

Randi hung the backpack on the back of the porch chair and turned to Davie. "Why are you here?" She hadn't meant for the question to come out so harshly. She was just used to being irritated with the man, and she'd had years to hone the feeling. "I mean, I didn't think you were coming over until Friday."

He stuffed his fingers in the front pockets of his jeans and looked everywhere but at her.

Damn the man! She could tell from his expression he was happy he'd flustered her. He stood and stalked toward her like he used to do when they were younger. Heat washed along her nerve endings and longing scrambled her brain.

She took a step toward him before she caught herself. Stuffing the puppy into his arms, she hurried into the house. The screen door slammed behind her as she strode toward the kitchen.

The hinges on the old screen squeaked then it slammed again as Davie entered after her. "I wanted to talk to you about the wedding. This has all been done in such a rush, I wanted to make sure everything is exactly the way you'd dreamed." He stood with the puppy tucked under one arm, his body a dark shadow in the sun's glare that flooded through the door. "You deserve everything you want and more."

Randi pulled in a deep breath and let it out slowly. She made her way to the couch and sank down. Unconsciously, she began tracing the lightening-shaped crack in the Naugahyde with her fingertip.

Davie followed her and set Tripper on the floor.

Closing her eyes, Randi tried to get enough space to think. Her brain seemed to shut down whenever she looked at Davie. "I think we should go through everything we've planned and make sure it's perfect for both of us. And thank you. I thought I didn't care what the ceremony and reception would be like, but this may be the only wedding I'll ever have."

Davie leaned back and waited. When the puppy whined, he reached down and lifted the little fluffy red and white dog to his lap.

Tripper circled and lay down with a sigh.

Randi smiled. Davie had always had a soft spot in his heart for animals.

When he raised his gaze to meet hers, he grinned. "I'm listening."

"First up is food," she said. "Three River's Barbeque is providing the main dishes."

"Check." Davie held up one finger.

The caterer is providing the desserts and salads."

"Check." Two fingers up.

"We have an appointment with the bakery to make the final decision on the wedding cake this afternoon."

"And again, check."

"Mavis, Camille, Christina, and Lucy have agreed to clean up the ranch for the wedding and reception."

"Got it." All four fingers were held in the air in front of Davie's face.

"And my wedding dress is altered and ready to go." The sleek dress made her feel like the perfect bride, and she'd fallen in love with the hand-beaded headband and short veil Mavis and Lucy had made. Too bad this wasn't for real.

"I think I should double check that one for myself."

Randi laughed out loud. "Before you start helping me, I have a question. Have you asked anyone to be your groomsmen? Mavis has agreed to be my matron of honor, and Christina and Camille are my bridesmaids."

"Dex, Drew, Rafe are participating under protest."

"Is Mr. Hughes going to make you all wear tuxedos? I can't see you in cutaway coats and tails." She closed her eyes for a moment trying to bring up that mental picture. The four men would look unbelievable in anything they wore, but she preferred jeans and jackets.

"If I don't get to see your dress, you don't get to see my wedding duds until the big day." He grinned as if he had a big surprise.

"Okay. So that's it, right?" She collapsed back onto the cracked vinyl of the sofa. "I'm tired already, and we haven't even gotten to the hard part."

"There's something harder than what we've already been through?"

"Yes, the wedding! Standing up in front of all those people pretending to be in love." She wouldn't be pretending, but she wouldn't let him know that.

He grinned his melt your heart grin as he took her hand. "At least the honeymoon will be easy. It's been a long time since we practiced that, but they say it's just like riding a bike."

The heat that had been building turned to ice in her veins. For a moment, she'd let herself forget why she and

65

Davie were together.

Randi leaped to her feet and ran down the hall. After locking her bedroom door, she threw herself onto the bed. How in the world was she ever going to get through this without losing her heart? Without losing her mind?

Losing Davie had nearly broken her the first time. She couldn't do it again. Pulling the pillow over her head to cover the sounds of her crying, she didn't answer when Davie knocked. Talking over this particular subject was off limits.

"Randi, I was just joking." His knock grew louder as did his voice. He rattled the knob. "If you don't open the door, I'll find another way in."

She held her breath, trying to stop the tears. Lifting the pillow, she listened. The room was silent. There was no knocking or yelling, the only sound the birds singing.

Had Davie left? If so, it was probably for the best. She wiped her eyes on the sheet and flopped back onto the bed. The screech of wood on wood shot her into a sitting position. Someone was prying off her window screen and sliding the window open.

Damn, damn, damn!

She never locked her bedroom windows. A house fire when she'd been ten had cured her of that. The utter panic of trying to open the window while the room filled with smoke had only faded a bit over the years.

Leave it to Davie to remember that little bit of information. The man knew entirely too much about her. He was the one person she'd told all her secrets—all but one.

At the sight of Davie's self-satisfied smile she fired her pillow at his head.

He batted it away then hoisted himself through the window and dropped to the floor. Picking up the pillow, he walked to the bed.

The sight of him sneaking in her bedroom window had set her heart racing. She still wanted him, had never stopped wanting him. She could dream about Davie, but she knew she couldn't have him.

For some reason she'd never figured out, life pulled the rug out from under her whenever she found something or someone she loved. In her heart, she knew she couldn't keep this cowboy.

The smirk on his face faded as he settled onto the bed beside her. "I obviously hit one of your buttons—maybe all of them." When she didn't answer, he continued. "Randi, I'm sorry. We don't have to go on a honeymoon. We'll just plead work overload."

#

As he sank onto the mattress, Davie had watched Randi shift as far away as she could without falling off the bed. This was the same bed she'd had when she'd lived at home, the same bed they'd shared. The memories of what they'd done in this bed heated his blood.

He watched the shifting emotions play across her face and knew he had his work cut out for him if he was ever going to regain her trust. Reaching out, he took her hand, running his thumb across her palm. "I'll never hurt you."

The sadness in her expression nearly broke his heart. He'd done this to her. By his selfish act, he'd nearly broken the strongest woman he'd ever known.

And being Lucy Dunbar's grandson, he was an expert on strong women.

"I'm sure you mean that. Right here, right now, you are certain you won't, but time has a way of changing things. "She carefully worked her hand out of his. In a movement that surprised him, she reached out and touched his face. "I'm pretty sure you don't remember saying those exact words years ago, but I do."

She was wrong about that. He remembered!

He'd tried running. He'd tried drinking. He'd tried everything he could think of to forget Randi, but without her, happiness didn't exist.

And, it was becoming clearer that she couldn't be happy with him.

"I remember. I remember everything about you, about us. I was a stupid kid. I only hope one day you can forgive me." He watched as she shifted a little farther away. He could see she wasn't ready. "How about this? I will do everything I can to make this wedding and the next six months go as smoothly as possible. I give you my word that when we're done, if you still feel the same, I'll leave, and you won't have to see me again."

Her nod was slow and careful. "You mean that?"

He meant it. The thought of never seeing Randi again was almost unthinkable, but if this was the only thing he could give her, he would. "Yes."

"Okay, then. Where were we?"

She was changing the subject, and he was going to let her, or they'd never make it through this mess. "When do we have to be at the bakery?"

"We need to leave now."

The hour drive to Boise was spent mostly in silence. He wondered what kind of goofy, frilly cake these people would have thought up.

"Bet you five dollars the cake will have white frosting and pastel flowers around the layers. To keep with the western theme, Mr. Hughes might have them put spurs on top."

"With the way our luck has been going with the show's contractors, I'd be a fool to take that bet."

He held the door to the bakery open and followed her inside. The aroma of freshly baked cakes and pastries filled the small space, and his stomach growled. At the sound of the bell when they entered, a middle-aged woman came out from the back room. "May I help you?"

"I'm Davie Dunbar, and this is Randi Bachmann. We have an appointment."

"Pleased to meet you both. I'm Connie Compton.

Have a seat, and I'll bring out the samples I've prepared."

Davie and Randi sat at the bar. "Sure you don't want to make a bet?"

"I'm sure." Randi picked up the cut glass pitcher and poured them each a glass of ice water. "I have to admit, I'm excited to see what Connie has to show us.

Ms. Compton brought out a white miniature cake with yellow frosting flowers scattered among the real pansies on the top and sides. "We call this, Bursting Into Spring. It's vanilla cake with raspberry filling and lemon frosting." She cut a piece and handed each one of them a fork. "What do you think?"

Randi took one bite then a second. "This is very pretty, and the taste is out of this world, but the design isn't really what I was thinking of."

When Connie looked at him, Davie nodded at Randi. "What she said." The smile that spread across Randi's face made his heart beat like snare drum at a marching band festival. He reached out and took her hand.

Connie sat with them and took out a pen and paper. "Why don't you tell me what you do want?"

"I don't know if you do this, but I'd like it to have a cowboy theme, but not hokey western. It would be so cool if the frosting weren't white. I like turquoise, but I don't know if I'd like a whole cake that color." Randi looked at Davie. "What do you want?"

He had no idea what he wanted in a cake. He'd opened his mouth to tell Randi to get anything she liked, when a thought occurred to him. "I don't care what the cake looks like. I'll go with whatever Randi decides, but I'd like to have one of Randi's buckles and one of mine on it if possible, and my parents have a china figurine of a man and a woman on horseback kissing. They got it as a wedding present from my grandmother. Can we use it as the topper?"

"We can do that." Connie tapped her fingers on the counter then grinned. "Wait here." She hurried away and came back with a rectangular cake. Brown frosting that looked like tooled leather contrasted nicely with turquoise accents. Edible silver Conchos and copper studs decorated the edges. Happy Birthday was written across the top. "Something like this?"

Randi smiled and Davie nodded. "Yes, but we'll need something bigger."

"The production team has already given me the number of guests. We'll have a three-tiered cake and two more sheet cakes." Connie took the cake back and came out with a tray of small sample cakes. "Try a bite of these and tell me which flavor you like best."

They decided on alternating layers of vanilla and chocolate with raspberry and vanilla filling. Connie packed up the remains of the small cakes in pale blue bakery boxes. "I'm going to try something new. If you can come back in a couple of days, I'll have a sample cake for you to look at."

"It's going to be hard for us to make it back." Davie looked at Randi. "Do we trust her?"

"Yes. You have a feel for what we want. Go ahead and make the cake and I'm sure we'll love it." Randi picked up the two boxes, and Davie followed her to the truck.

When they'd hit the freeway, Davie turned down the radio. "Are you still good with all this? The wedding is only eight days away." The panic level in his gut was growing, as the event got closer. He wasn't completely sure Randi wouldn't back out, and this was his best bet to get her to marry him.

"I'm scared to death." Randi's usually stoic voice shook with emotion. "What if they find out? What if we hate each other every day of the six months we're married?"

Davie held his breath for a moment, trying to decide if he should speak his mind, but the only way they'd make it through this was if they were honest with each other. "What if we don't?"

"Don't?" Confusion deepened the lines between

Randi's eyes.

"What if we don't grow to hate each other? What if the opposite happens and we find love again?"

"You'd want that?"

How was he going to answer her question without blowing her away with his eagerness? Well, he was the one who thought honest was the best way to go. "Yes."

"I'm sorry Davie. I can marry you. I can live with you as long as we have some rules. I think I can even like you, but I can't love you. It hurt too much."

CHAPTER SEVEN

Randi's stomach twisted and turned like a wild steer on the end of a buckaroo's rope. If she'd thought the production crew wouldn't chase her down, she'd have jumped back into her truck and raced away.

She'd arrived at the ranch at six a.m. for the shooting of the "extra footage" as Mr. Hughes called it. They didn't shoot until ten, but Hughes had insisted they needed to fix her hair and makeup.

As the make-up artist and stylist had bustled around her, she hadn't bothered looking in the mirror. She seldom wore makeup and a braid was her everyday hairstyle. At this point, she'd almost given up fighting Mr. Hughes.

She had no idea what the extra footage involved. Hughes had insisted on keeping it a secret. He'd said he didn't want them practicing their answers. "The television viewers love real reactions."

Randi had pasted a smile on her face to keep from strangling the man. The only games she enjoyed playing were slot machines.

Just as the makeup artist led her out of Mavis and Dex's, Davie wandered over from the old house. In his western shirt and Wranglers, he looked good enough to eat. His go-to-town boots glowed with a recent shine, and his black Stetson was dust free. He carried a handmade rawhide rope, one of his Dad's favorite bridles, and a pair of chinks.

Dropping the armload on the ground, he moved to stand beside Randi.

"Are we all ready to have fun?" Mr. Hughes put an arm around Randi and Davie's shoulders. His smiling face was tight with tension today.

"You two might, but I'm not sure I'm going to have any fun at all." Randi watched Mr. Hughes's expression change as he tried to figure out if she was joking.

I'm probably the most reluctant bride he's ever had on the show.

The man cleared his throat. "Let's get started, shall we?" He pointed to an area by the barn where the crew had constructed a stage that looked a lot like the set of any number of game shows. There was a solid cherry wood lectern in the center with an inlaid pine heart on the front.

To each side were smaller painted podiums, one pink and one blue. Someone had fixed Davie's rope to the front of the blue one, a bridle with a spade bit hung from one corner, and two pairs of cowboy boots nestled against the bottom. A wreath of baby's breath and tiny roses hung on the front of the pink one, with a bride's veil and sparkly shoes in place of the bridle and cowboy boots. Randi walked to the blue one and stood behind it. "I call dibs on this one."

Mr. Hughes' normally pale face turned bright red. "No, no, no!" He stopped talking and pulled in a deep breath. When he had control, he walked over to Randi. "Please move over to the other one. It's for the bride."

"But I don't want the fru fru one. I'm more of a buckaroo type of girl."

"I really have to put my foot down on this. We've given in to most of your requests—"

"Because they made your show better." Randi felt her temper begin to overtake her good sense. She bit the inside of her cheek in an effort to stop.

Davie pulled her into his arms and whispered in her ear. "I was pretty sure you'd have a problem with this. Leave this to me. You're going to love the set-up when I'm done." He trailed a line of soft kisses down her neck then moved away to the pile of things he'd brought from the house.

In minutes, he'd replaced the wreath with the rawhide. Nana Lucy tucked a large Peace rose into the coils.

Mavis stepped forward to help. She wove the veil through the bridle and hung the chinks from the other side of the pink lectern.

With a grin bright enough to light the ranch on a cloudy day, Davie looked at her. "This is more your style."

Randi hurried over to the reconfigured podium. It was Davie's dad's bridle and rawhide rope, but those were her grandfather's chinks. Davie must have snuck them out of her house. She whirled and wrapped her arms around his neck. "Thank you."

Mr. Hughes still carried a fair amount of tension, but he wasn't yelling anymore. "Can you each take your place?"

With no way to get out of this, Randi walked to the pink podium. She kept reminding herself that this was a means to an end. A way to get what she wanted. A way to rodeo and rope and own her own place.

She could be a bride, dammit.

Mr. Hughes blew into his microphone to get their attention. "Now before we begin, I'll explain how this works. First, when I ask—"

As Mr. Hughes talked on and on, Randi rolled her eyes.

Davie saw her and raised his eyebrows.

She rolled them again.

"Excuse me, Mr. Hughes. We need a minute."

Hughes waved his hand in permission. "Sure, don't mind us. We're not on any kind of schedule."

Davie took Randi's hand and led her around the edge

of the barn. He placed a hand on each of her cheeks and kissed her lips.

This was more like it. She'd stay here all day.

"You can do this. I watched as you worked your fingers to the bone learning to goat tie and breakaway rope. You practiced until you were the best around. Compared to that, this is easy. All you have to do is act like you love me." Davie pulled her in for a hug then stepped back.

"But I don't love you. I can't."

He took a sharp breath and let it out in a sigh. "Randi, you can pretend." The smile he'd maintained all day dropped away, and he stared at the ground. "Do you want to call this off now?"

"No!" The word burst out of her with the force of a hurricane. She cleared her throat. "I mean, no. We both need the money, and you're right, I can do this. I've been throwing a big pity party for myself for no reason. It's not like someone is killing my dog. It's just a game."

As she turned back to the crew, she heard Davie mutter. "Not for me."

"What?"

Heat rose in his cheeks, but the transformation from dejected to cocky happened in a flash. "Win for me. I bet Dex I could talk you into this."

She studied him for a moment, but whatever he'd been thinking had been washed away by sheer determination. "Nice save." She walked away before this got even more awkward.

In the center of her podium was a bright, red button. When she pushed it, a buzzer sounded.

Hughes had given up trying to act like she was a normal bride. "Stop that!" He'd have been perfect in the role of an angry schoolteacher in an old western.

Randi gave him the grin she used just before she rode in the roping box at the rodeos and hit the button again. "Yes, Mr. Hughes."

When they were in their places and the cameras were

set just right, Mr. Hughes smiled and introduced them to the future television audience. "The guests of honor on *Your Dream Wedding* today are Miranda Bachmann and David Dunbar."

"Davie," Randi said. When the camera turned to her Randi grinned and waved. She felt like a fool, but if this was what they were paying her for, she'd give them her best.

"What?" Mr. Hughes voice cut through the silence. If the cameras hadn't been rolling, she was sure he'd have had a few choice words for her. "Cut!" He turned to Randi, his eyebrows raised, and his lips pressed into a thin line.

"Davie isn't a nickname. It's on his birth certificate."

He stared at her for a long minute before looking at the stack of notes on his lectern. "Roll cameras." With an effort, Hughes smiled at the camera. "Well then, let me introduce Davie Dunbar and Miranda Bachmann. It will be obvious to our regular viewers that we're playing our version of the Newlywed Game. We like to call it Nearly Newlywed. I'll ask a question, and the first one to hit the buzzer will get to answer. You get a point for each right answer." He glanced from Randi to Davie. "If there's a discrepancy in your answers, your friends and family have agreed to act as tie-breakers."

Randi nodded, as did Davie.

"The first set of questions is about both of you." Mr. Hughes straightened the cards on the podium. He picked up the top one and with a flourish read the question. "How did you first meet?"

Randi thought for a moment then pushed her button. A loud buzz filled the air.

"How did you meet David?" Mr. Hughes asked.

Randi smiled into the camera. "I don't know anyone named David, but I met my Davie at a junior rodeo when we were ten. Mavis introduced us." Even before she'd finished talking she saw Davie shaking his head. "What?

You know that's how we met."

Davie continued to shake his head.

"Alright, when do you think we met?" She kept her gaze fixed to Davie.

"It was when we were seven at dance lessons."

Hell's Bells, he was right. Her mother had made her take the lessons in an effort to make a lady out of her. It hadn't worked. The dance instructor had asked her to leave after three weeks when she'd refused to learn the steps to the waltz or rumba.

Both her mother and the instructor had wanted her to act like the other little girls, and she couldn't do that. She'd been more of a free spirit, and after being kicked out, she'd erased everything about those dance lessons from her memory.

#

"Do you want to dispute Davie's answer?" The cameras rolled as they waited for her reply.

Randi shook her head no. "I hate to admit it, but he's right. I'll get the next one though. You can bet on that." Davie took in her determined expression. Just put Randi into a competition, any kind of competition, and she went balls to the wall. She thrived on winning.

"Miss Taffy." Mr. Hughes turned his attention to the young woman standing beside the reader board.

She smiled brightly. In her short denim skirt, red paisley Daisy Duke blouse, and tourist stand cowboy hat Davie wondered if she'd come straight from an auto parts calendar shoot. This must be the costume department's idea of western.

"Taffy, please put up one point for our groom." Turning back to the camera Hughes asked the next question. "What did you eat on your first date?"

Randi's head jerked up, and she slammed her hand down on the buzzer. "Rodeo burgers and fries."

Davie waited for Mr. Hughes to look at him. He shook his head no.

"What do you mean no? We always ate rodeo burgers when we were done competing." She stood stiffly with her hands braced on the top of the podium, the very essence of pissed-off woman.

His pissed-off woman if he had anything to say about it. He shook his head again, enjoying this game more and more. "We did eat burgers when we were done roping, but those weren't dates. The first time I took you out on a real date, we went to the Hong Kong Restaurant in Nampa after the last performance of the Snake River Stampede." He waited as the memory caught up with her.

"No, I'm right about this one. It's got to be the rodeo burgers. We ate a lot of them before you ever took me out."

Mr. Hughes broke in. "Do you want to dispute Davie's answer?"

"Yes, yes I do." She turned to the people in the chairs lined up in front of them, giving a wave to her friends. "Tell him I'm right."

Dex and Mavis, Lucy and Rafe talked among themselves and then Mavis stood. "I get to be the spokesman—make that spokes-cowgirl because Dex and Rafe say I talk all the time."

If the outcome of her friend's vote hadn't meant the difference between winning and losing this damned game, Randi would have laughed out loud. There had been years when Mavis had hardly spoken a word. Everything had changed when she and Dex had gotten back together again.

Mavis turned and stuck out her tongue at the others before facing Randi again. "We'd love to agree with you, Randi, but Davie's right. Every time we ate rodeo burgers, we were just a group of friends. Those weren't dates."

"I can't believe my best friend would desert me on this." Randi turned back to Mr. Hughes. "Give me the next question."

Mr. Hughes struggled to contain his smile. "Taffy, please put up another point for the groom." He shuffled the top card to the bottom and picked up the next. "For those of you who haven't kept up, the score is two points for the groom, and—let's see. Zero points for the bride."

Randi opened her mouth, but Davie caught her eye and shook his head.

With a sigh, she leaned against the podium and waited.

"We'll move to the questions about favorites. Will each of you write the name of your favorite cow pony on the card in front of you and hand it to Taffy?" The Dukes of Hazzard wanna-be gathered the cards and moved to stand next to Mr. Hughes.

"Now, Randi, tell us which horse Davie thinks is the best one he's ever owned."

"There's only one answer to this one. Davie's favorite was his heading horse when we were in college. His name was Big Al, and Davie loved him more than anything or anyone."

"Never more than you." And he'd done it again. Opened his mouth when he should have just smiled.

Randi grasped the edges of the podium with her hands and leaned back on her heels. After a moment of staring at the ground, she directed her gaze at Davie. "Am I right?"

Mr. Hughes held up Davie's card. It read, *Al.* "Is this the same horse?"

Davie nodded. "Best horse I ever threw a leg over."

Mr. Hughes didn't seem nearly as happy about asking Taffy to put up one point for the bride. "Now Davie. Tell us which is Randi's best horse."

"I don't know if this is what she said, but it has to be Contrary, because the ornery old bugger taught her to ride and train." He wasn't sure if she'd pick the paint mare she'd ridden in high school or not, but in his mind, Contrary had forced Randi to up her game. Together they'd won the district High School Rodeo State championship in breakaway three times and heeling once.

Mr. Hughes held up the card. It read *Drummer*.

Randi looked shell shocked. She held up her hand like she was in grade school. "Mr. Hughes? To be honest, I didn't think about Contrary. I think maybe Davie's right."

Davie had a mental picture of Randi and the mare. They'd been unstoppable until a bowed tendon had put an end to their partnership. Davie had held Randi as she'd cried for hours the day she'd sold Contrary to a young girl who wanted to trail ride. It was the only reasonable choice, but Randi had been inconsolable.

"As much as I'd like to let you change your favorite, the rules say the answers have to match on the first try. The score is two for the groom and two for the bride." The cameraman panned over to the scoreboard then back to Mr. Hughes. "One more question. Now pay attention because you both have a chance to win the contest. Are you ready?"

Randi bounce on her feet like she was warming up for a physical competition. "Yes."

He held up the next card and read. "Soon you'll be man and wife. Next is a family. When your first child is born, will it look like you, Randi?" He gave Randi a practiced smile before turning to Davie. "Or will it look like you, Davie?"

Davie shifted his attention from Mr. Hughes to Randi.

He caught a glimpse of tears filling her eyes before she dropped her gaze to her hands. They'd never talked about the pregnancy or how he'd reacted.

When Randi had called and asked him to drive out to Leslie Gulch, he'd assumed she was looking forward to some alone time. He sure as hell had been.

They'd always joked that the desert gods had painted the towering cliffs at the gulch in desert hues and constructed the mysterious honeycombed walls and unique rock formations just for them. In truth, the area was made of ash from several volcano calderas many millions of years ago.

But playing around had not been on her agenda that day. When she'd told him she was pregnant, he'd been stunned.

He hadn't been ready to become a father. Hell, he could barely take care of himself. As Randi had stood there, hope in her eyes, he hadn't said a word, just stared at the ground until she told him to get back in the truck.

Neither one said a word as Randi drove him to the ranch. He'd climbed out of her truck without a word and hurried into the house.

He could only imagine what he'd looked like, because Dex, his father and his grandmother all asked him what was wrong.

He hadn't told anyone, and when Randi called a couple of days later to tell him she'd been wrong about the baby, he'd hit the road and run as far and as fast as he could.

"Do you need me to repeat the question?" Mr. Hughes' voice held a note of impatience.

Randi stood frozen in place, all the color drained from her face. She stared at her hands, her body shaking, and Davie felt like hitting something or someone. He couldn't let this go on. "We need to stop!"

"We've only got this question. Surely you can make it for another five minutes." Mr. Hughes frowned, but Davie had been raised by Lucy Dunbar, and he didn't intimidate easily.

"Well, yeah sure. But I'm going to throw up, and I'm pretty sure you don't want that all over your nice set here." Davie strode over and took hold of Randi's hand, pulling her toward the house.

Normally, if he'd tried to force her to do anything, she'd have fought him like a badger cub. This time, he knew she was upset because she followed meekly behind.

Inside the house, he pulled her into his arms. "I'm sorry. I didn't know they were going to ask that."

She nodded into his shirt. "It caught me off guard, is

all."

Davie rested his chin on the top of her head. "I never asked you what happened. Did me being such an ass cause you to lose the baby?"

She stiffened then pulled back. Walking across the room, she turned to face him. "No. I lost my baby because I'm so damned determined to prove to the world I'm the toughest woman alive."

STEPHANIE BERGET

CHAPTER EIGHT

There, she'd said it. She'd said it out loud. She'd told Davie that she'd as much as killed their baby. And she didn't want to talk about it anymore. She started for the door.

Davie caught her hand and led her to a kitchen chair. He pulled another one up so close their knees touched. "I know without a doubt you didn't have an abortion. At the time I thought that might be an option, but I knew even then you wouldn't go along with that. After I thought about it, I knew I couldn't either. Now, why don't you explain?"

"I lost the baby and you left. There's nothing more to say."

"You told me—"

They heard a soft knock on the back door, and Lucy entered. "That know-it-all out there wants you back on the set. He keeps ranting on about filming schedules and costs per hour." She stood, hands on her hips, her toe tapping against the linoleum, and Randi knew Lucy was waiting for them to turn her loose on Mr. Hughes.

Before either of them could say a word, Mr. Hughes stood towering over Davie's grandmother. "We need you out here right now. If you throw up, we'll cut it out of the footage."

"We're done for the day," Davie said, standing too close to Mr. Hughes. "We'll try another day with another question."

Mr. Hughes sputtered. "Look, if we don't get this done today, we'll be behind schedule. If your segment isn't ready to go on time, the deal is off. You won't get the money."

They both needed the money. They'd gone through a lot to get to this point. She could answer the question now that she'd had time to prepare. She'd just say it would be a boy and look like his father. She opened her mouth, but Davie cut her off.

"Take your money and your cameras and your show and shove—"

"Davie." She waited until he looked at her. "It's okay."

"No, it's not. We're done for the day." He turned toward Mr. Hughes. "You can set up another day to film or we'll cancel the whole thing, and you can keep the money."

"Now, don't get hasty. I'm sure we can work things out."

"You do what you have to do." Davie took her hand and led her to the truck. As he drove along the gravel road leading from the ranch, she watched him. He was handsome for sure, he always had been, but something had changed.

His jaw was set and his brows pulled together into a dangerous looking frown. The question had really upset him, but she wasn't ready to bring up the subject of the show. "Where are we going?"

He turned his head and gave her a small smile. "Someplace I think you'll like."

It didn't take long for Randi to figure out their destination.

Leslie Gulch.

Fixing her gaze out the side window, she concentrated

on regaining control of her emotions. She'd always loved the wild, unique feel of Leslie Gulch, but she hadn't been down this road since the day she'd told Davie she was pregnant.

As he pulled into a wide turnout across from the tall, multi-colored spires that were their favorite landmark, she sighed. "I wasn't sure if I wanted to come back here, but I'm glad we did. This place always calms my soul."

Davie kept his eyes trained on her as she spoke. When she looked at him, he didn't smile. "Tell me about the baby."

She could have spun the tale a million ways, but not telling the whole truth had put her in this predicament. No way could she look at him. She picked at the cuticle on her right thumb. "You didn't want it."

"I was scared." Davie climbed out of the truck and came around to the passenger side and opened the door.

"So was I, but after I realized you weren't interested in getting married, I decided I could raise it myself." She stopped, took a deep breath and took his hand. "So I called and told you I'd lost it."

He jerked back, his eyes wide. "You didn't? What the hell, Randi! That's my child, too. Did you put it up for adoption?" He walked away then stormed back. "Never mind that. Was it a boy or girl?"

She saw the hope in his face, and her heart stuttered in her chest. "After you left, I was determined to prove to myself and everyone else that I was tough enough. I took in a horse for training that I shouldn't have. Several other trainers had turned the gelding down, but that didn't stop me. He bucked me off." When she tried to laugh, it came out as a raw, sorrowful croak. "The damned thing threw me over the fence, and I landed in that pile of firewood we split before you left. Two days later, I had a miscarriage."

"That was a dumb thing to do, but we've all done dumb things." Davie nudged her over on the bench seat and settled beside her. "It wasn't your fault."

"The doctor said I might have lost the baby anyway. Getting bucked off might not have had anything to do with the miscarriage, but I know. It was my stupid actions that cost our child its life."

After pushing at him until he got out of the truck, she hurried away. The reservoir was less than two miles ahead. Maybe by the time she got there, she'd have figured out what to do about the mess she'd made of her life.

Not likely. She'd been trying to figure that out for six years. For a woman who at one time had had her whole life planned out, she'd become the screw-up champion of the world.

The large boulder sitting next to the road had probably been there for a million years. She climbed to the top and pulled her knees up, wrapping her arms around her legs. The day was warm and the air filled with the scent of hot dust and sage. Thoughts flitted through her mind at warp speed.

She'd always thought she could tame any horse and wrestle any problem to the ground if she just tried hard enough. With Davie, life had been an adventure. Without him, it had become a struggle to survive.

"Are you okay?"

By the time Davie found her, her tears had dried, but the questions still flourished.

She looked into his clear blue eyes. "Was it me? Would you have been happy about having a baby with someone else? Someone who was more ladylike, more nurturing?" That was a question she'd asked herself many times over the years.

He crawled up beside her. When he pulled her close, she lay down with her head on his lap.

She closed her eyes and relaxed as Davie stroked his fingers through her hair.

"Randi, I have never loved anyone but you. When you brought me out here, I thought you wanted to have sex. I was a kid, and that was pretty much all that was on my mind twenty-four seven. I wasn't prepared to be a dad. Hell, I thought my dad was a jerk and wasn't sure I could do better." He massaged her neck and arm. "After I had time to think, I knew we could be better parents than ours were. I was trying to get up enough courage to tell you when you told me you'd lost the baby."

She rolled over enough to see his face. "You're just telling me that to make me feel better."

He did manage a smile this time. "No, I'm not, and when you told me you weren't pregnant any more, I decided to get the hell out. I knew I couldn't keep my hands off you if I stayed, and sooner or later, there might be another baby."

"You were probably right about that. We never were very good at stopping our impulses." She remembered the all-encompassing feeling of being loved when she'd been in Davie's arms. Kind of like the feeling she had right now. "Kiss me."

The setting sun blazed through a crack in the stone tower above them, bathing them both in warmth. Davie leaned over and pressed his lips to hers, and for the first time in a long time, Randi's world was right.

#

The drive from the Gulch to Randi's house took a day and a half, or at least it seemed that way to Davie. If he hadn't learned some self-control over the years, he'd have taken her in the back seat of his truck, but she deserved better than that.

They'd started shedding clothes even before they'd reached the front door. It was a good thing her house didn't have any close neighbors.

"Good thing you got Tripper's kennel done, or we'd be tripping over a puppy." Randi grinned as she leaned against the wall in the hallway. She didn't break eye contact as she pulled off one boot and then the other, dropping them to the floor with a thump. "Catch me if you can."

Davie toed his off as she ran to the bedroom. "Hey, wait for me!"

As he stepped into the doorway, she held up a hand. "Stop!"

His worst fear was coming true. She'd had time to think about what they were going to do and had changed her mind.

He leaned against the wall. Keeping his hands off Randi might be the hardest thing he'd ever done, but this was her call. "Do you want me to leave?"

She ran her hands behind her neck and lifted her hair. The strands flowed off her fingers like chocolate silk. "No, I don't want you to leave. I want you to stand right there until I tell you to move." Popping the button on her jeans, she hummed the Stripper song, as she shimmied out of her pants.

When the snaps on her shirt flew open, and the shirt sailed across the room, his heart nearly stopped in his chest.

The amount of effort it took to keep from running across the room and throwing Randi on the bed was almost more than he could bear. He folded his arms across his chest in an effort to appear unaffected.

She just grinned. Hooking a finger beneath one strap of her white cotton bra, she slid it down. When he went to take a step toward her, she shook her head. "Ah, ah, ah. You aren't supposed to move yet." The second strap slid down her tanned arm.

Hell!

When she popped the front clasp, the tiny bit of cloth slid to the floor. That did it. His self-control wasn't only gone, it had been blasted into the next county. Closing the distance between them in two steps, he pulled her into his arms.

"Wait, I'm not done." Her giggles set him on fire.

"Oh yes you are. I can take care of anything else." He

put his hands on her waist and lifted her onto the bed. "I'll show you."

Randi tried to scramble away, but he caught her foot. "Where are you going?" Davie pulled her beneath him and caged her in his arms. Her beautiful face glowed, and her skin was as soft as he remembered.

"I was going to help you undress."

"You got to do your dance. Don't you think it's my turn?"

"But I'm just an amateur, and you, sir, are a professional. I don't think I can afford your dance." She ran her hands down both legs and peeked beneath her lacy underwear as if searching for pockets. "It seems I've misplaced my money."

Davie almost laughed out loud. They used to play around all the time like this, and he'd missed it. He rolled off the bed and unsnapped the top of his Wranglers. "I have a new act. If you're good, I'll let you critique it before I take it on the road."

He pushed his jeans and underwear to the floor and stepped out before pulling off his shirt. As he walked around the bed, watching her, he saw her eyes go wide.

"Oh, my, sir. That is quite an act you've got there. It's sure to be a hit with the ladies."

"There's only one lady who's going to see it, and I hope she's impressed." The scent that was Randi filled this room, sweet and spicy with a hint of cinnamon. He couldn't wait to sink into her and find his way home.

Randi's playfulness faded. She reached for his hand and pulled him onto the bed. "She is, and always has been."

Davie stroked a fingertip around one nipple and then the other. He looked up to see Randi watching him. Her skin pebbled as he ran his hand down her ribcage to her stomach.

As he moved it lower, she gasped. "Now, Davie." Spreading her legs, she wrapped them around his hips.

This woman had captured his heart in dance class when

they'd been seven, and she'd never let go. They settled into a rhythm as old as time, and he felt the tension building in her body.

I love you. I love you. I love you! His brain screamed the words he longed to say, but he'd already told her, and she hadn't answered.

As she climaxed, he heard her whisper. "I love you." That was all he needed.

When he'd first left home, he'd foolishly thought he'd find another love.

Stupid cowboy.

After years of searching, he realized there wasn't another woman in the world that made him feel like Randi.

He held her in his arms for the rest of the night, content for the first time since he'd run from responsibility.

As the sun rose, Randi rolled over and laid her chin on his chest, wrapping her arms around his body. "Good thing my horses are on pasture. I would have forgotten to feed them last night. Guess I had something else on my mind."

"I hope you don't expect me to remind you. I was a bit pre-occupied, too." Davie watched as she grinned and climbed out of bed.

Gathering up the empty condom wrappers, she disappeared into the bathroom. At the sound of water running, he decided taking a shower right now was a must.

Steam filled the shower as water coursed down her body. Randi's silky skin gleamed in the morning light. Beautiful and soft and it was all his. That thought stopped him. He turned her to face him. "Are you okay with this?"

She pushed the wet hanks of hair out of her face and frowned. "Didn't I act okay? You don't think you coerced me into having sex with you, do you? I don't coerce or don't you remember?"

She stood under the streaming water, her hands on her hips, and he didn't think he'd ever seen a more beautiful creature. "No. No." He shook his head trying to clear his mind. Nothing he said right now would be right. "I caught myself thinking about the future, and it occurred to me that the future might not be what you had in mind."

"You mean after the fake wedding?" She relaxed, and just as he was about to hear the answer to his question, she shrieked and jumped out of the tub.

As he turned to question her, he felt icy water hit his back. The hot water heater had lost it's hot.

Randi dug into the old cabinet and threw a towel to him before getting one of her own. "My bedroom is warmer," she said as she hurried away.

"I found that out last night." Davie followed her like a puppy on a leash. He dried off and pulled on his Wranglers. "You didn't answer my question. Is this an itch you need scratched or something more permanent?" He rubbed the towel through his hair then ran his fingers through it.

Randi pulled her old plaid bathrobe out of the closet and slipped into it as he waited impatiently for her answer.

She stood looking at him, the robe open. Her eyes filled with tears. "I still don't know if it's a mistake, but I love you. If I hadn't taken things into my own hands—if I'd trusted you . . . If I hadn't lied to you, we might be married now with a baby. No, with a kindergartener."

She flew into his arms, crying and laughing and kissing him over and over.

Davie held her as tight as he could. "Just so we're on the same page."

CHAPTER NINE

Although Randi had assured Davie it would be okay, he'd convinced Mr. Hughes to replace the baby question with a less disturbing one. They'd finished filming and wrapped up all the little details with three whole days to spare.

On a trip to Caldwell, they'd driven by a mobile home showroom to window shop, and left the new owners of a triple-wide. On their next visit to the ranch, they found a perfect spot by the creek behind the Lucy's ranch house. Their only problem was the manufacturer needed three months before they could deliver the home.

So, for now, they'd stay in Randi's tiny rental.

Bright early summer sunshine warmed her back as she pulled the last weed from the tiny flowerbed by the back door. The sound of a hammer caught her attention as she dug a hole in the freshly tilled earth.

She looked up to see the muscles in Davie's back ripple beneath his skin as he nailed down some loose cedar shakes on the roof of the shed that housed her tack.

I wonder if he'd mind heading back to the bedroom.

Self-control had never been her strong suit when it came to Davie. If she didn't leave him alone the roof would never get done. She tucked a purple pansy into the dirt then rocked back on her heels.

She wasn't too upset at the long waiting period for their home to be delivered. This little house wasn't much, but at least she could watch the colorful blooms. And, they had all the privacy in the world here.

By the time the sun dipped below the horizon, they'd worked together to rehang the screen door so it didn't scrape along the wooden porch boards when it opened. Davie attached a chain on the back screen to prevent it from slamming into the side of the house when the wind blew.

Randi opened the back screen and let it go. It swung closed with a small thud. "Now, we'll have to buy an alarm system. I never had to worry before about someone breaking in. Whether the front or back, the doors made too much noise for anyone to be sneaky." She moved down the steps and picked up the hose, turning a gentle spray on the new flowers.

"Except, all a guy had to do was climb in your bedroom window." Davie peered at her through the screen.

"You are the only one who ever got away with that." She finished giving the last pansy a drink before turning the spray on Davie.

He slammed the door shut. When she'd turned off the water, he opened it a crack. "You do that again and you're going to make me angry."

Randi held both hands up, palms out. "Well, if one of us gets mad, you know what that means."

When he looked at her without answering, she continued. "Make-up sex."

Davie flew out the door and with a shriek, Randi raced around the house. She'd let him catch her eventually.

It was nearly dark by the time they had the tools put away and the horses' water checked. With a heaping plate of toasted tuna sandwiches, a bag of chips, and a carton of salsa they curled together in front of the television.

After they'd cleaned up the food, Randi leaned her head against Davie's shoulder and closed her eyes. The wedding prep had taken more out of her than she'd thought. As she drifted off to sleep, she realized this was her last night as an unmarried woman.

Her sleep was interrupted by a cacophony of horns coming from the front of the house. She joined Davie at the front window and saw two trucks and a car pulling up the driveway.

Mavis and Dex climbed out of their pickup, Rafe was in his old Dodge, and Lucy's little red car brought up the rear.

"Did you invite them over?" Davie turned to her.

"No, I was looking forward to our last night of living in sin." She smiled. A month ago, she'd never have imagined she'd be this happy, and with Davie.

Multiple fists pounded on the wooden door and voices called out.

"Guess we'd better let them in before they break down the door." Randi twisted the knob and stepped back.

Mavis and Lucy gave her a hug then disappeared down the hall.

"What the hell?" Davie looked from the hallway to Randi. "What's going on?"

She shrugged her shoulders before turning to Dex. "What have your wife and grandmother cooked up now?" His grin told her it was nothing good.

Dex threw a duffle bag at his brother, and Rafe laid a clothing bag across the back of the couch. "There, you're all set."

"All set for what?" Davie unzipped the duffel and peered inside. "I don't get it."

Mavis and Lucy came back into the living room with armloads of Randi's things. "I think we got everything. If we forgot anything essential, Dex can run down and get it for you."

Lucy handed the clothes she'd gathered to Rafe and took Randi's arm. "Come on, dear. It's getting late, and I need my beauty sleep."

Randi shrugged her off as gently as she could. "What is this? Why are you all here?"

Lucy patted her arm before taking her hand again. "You can't spend the night with your future husband the night before the wedding. It's bad luck."

"Yeah, and you'll be all worn out, and the honeymoon won't be nearly as much fun. At least that's what they tell me." Rafe's grin almost had Randi laughing.

She couldn't imagine the wedding night being anything but spectacular if the last few days were any indication. "I'm sorry you went to all this trouble, and we appreciate the sentiment, but we're not going anywhere."

At the look on Mavis' face, a nasty shiver ran down her back, and Dex's grin didn't make her feel any better.

"We thought you'd say that, so we all brought our jammies, and we'll stay here with you." Mavis started toward the door.

Lucy reached into her large handbag and pulled out a flannel nightgown. "See, I'm ready."

"Where are you going to sleep?" Randi only had one bed and the sofa.

"Lucy and I are going to confiscate your bed." Mavis put her arm around her mother-in-law's shoulder, and they both grinned.

"You can't ask an eighty something year old woman to sleep on the floor." Lucy smoothed the nightgown across the back of the couch.

"You already don't like me, so what difference does it make," Randi said to her almost grandmother-in-law. "You haven't said over four words to me since you found out we were getting married."

Lucy took Randi's hand. "That was before I realized you really loved my grandson. Love changes everything."

Randi had to agree with that.

Davie wrapped an arm around Randi and Lucy. "She's got a point. I think we'd better go along with these people. I know them all personally, and they can be dangerous when they think they're doing a good thing."

His kiss made Randi forget she was being kidnapped. Mavis and Dex pulled them apart, and Randi was shuttled out the door and into Rafe's truck.

Mavis buckled her seatbelt then patted the strap. "There you go."

"Trying to keep me safe?"

"Trying to keep you in the truck until Rafe is driving fast enough that you won't jump out." Mavis gave her a hug and slammed the door.

It was dark enough now that she could only see Rafe's outline. His deep voice came out of the darkness. "Sure you're okay with this?"

Was she? As she thought about his question, she realized she was. All of these people loved her and Davie enough to make the wedding something to remember. When their children were parents, this would still be a story told on holidays. "Yeah, I'm good."

The tiny sliver of the new moon provided very little light, and the darkness in the cab of the truck was nearly complete. Rafe seemed content in the silence, and Randi settled back and closed her eyes. For the first time in months, she relaxed.

Even when she thought of the upcoming ceremony, the panic she'd lived with since Christina had first mentioned *Your Dream Wedding* didn't appear. Soon she'd be Davie's partner for life, and she couldn't be more ready.

Going to the ranch was probably the best thing her friends could have forced her to do. A smile spread across her face. She'd never give them the satisfaction of knowing that though.

As they turned onto the gravel drive to the ranch house, Rafe cleared his throat. "I've only got one question."

Surely Rafe wouldn't want to get into why they were marrying or if she loved Davie. He couldn't possibly want to know what had prompted their break up years ago. She tried to keep her voice neutral. "What?"

"How long do you think it will take Davie to ditch Dex and walk to the ranch?"

#

"Oh, crap!" Davie dropped his cell phone onto the couch with a little more force than was necessary. Okay, okay! He threw it.

He'd tried to call Randi for over an hour last night. On the third call this morning, Mavis had answered.

"Good morning. Are you ready to get married?"

Her chirpy voice was irritating, made more so by the fact that he hadn't gotten much sleep. Randi's scent was everywhere in this little house, and the few times he'd fallen asleep, he'd dreamed she was next to him.

Waking up and finding out she was still gone was not the way he wanted to start his day. "Could I talk to Randi?"

"Well, normally I'd hand the phone to her, but it's your wedding day. You're just going to have to wait for the ceremony. Besides, she's still asleep." She must have put her hand over the phone because the sound of her laugh was muffled. "I'll talk to you later."

And she hung up on him. She hung up on him!

He wandered outside to find Dex brushing down Randi's old horse. Robins and Meadowlarks sang their hearts out, and bees buzzed around the rusty wheelbarrow Randi had filled with flowers. This would have been a picture perfect day if Randi had been here to share it with him.

"Isn't it about time to head to the ranch?"

Dex looked over his shoulder. "The ceremony is supposed to start at three. It's only seven a.m. My orders are to keep you here until one thirty, and I'm very good at following orders."

Davie snorted. "You, follow orders? Tell me another lie." He grabbed the pitchfork and cleaned up the area.

"You'll find out. It's not that I'm forced to follow orders, but I look things over and decide the best way to accomplish what I want. It isn't my fault if more often than not after I've thought things through, what I want is what Mavis wants."

For years, Dex had held their family together while Davie had moved around looking for himself and Drew had followed his songbird wife around the world. Dex had taken the responsibility seriously. It was good to see him relaxed and happy.

In Davie's opinion, the Dunbar brothers knew how to pick good women.

Well, two thirds of them did.

"So if I can't go find Randi, what should we do for the next six hours?"

"We can clean your truck. You'll be taking it to the airport, right?" Dex started toward the house, and Davie followed. "Hey, where is the show sending you on your honeymoon anyway?"

"I don't know. They wanted to keep it a secret, but the way they've planned most of this wedding, I'm a little scared." Davie opened the cupboard doors until he found several boxes of cereal.

Dex pulled open the refrigerator. "Hope she has fresh milk."

"She will. That woman lives on cereal." Davie grabbed bowls, and they each chose a box.

"Are you ready for the ceremony?" Dex spooned his mouth full of Frosted Flakes. As he swallowed, he lifted another bite to his mouth but stopped and looked at his brother. "I know this started out as a way to make money for you and Randi. That's changed, right?"

Davie set the bowl of Rice Krispies on the counter.

"The money has nothing to do with this. I'd marry Randi if I had to pay to do it."

"Does she feel the same way?" Dex's brows drew down into a frown.

Suddenly Davie wasn't hungry. He poured the remaining cereal into the puppy's bowl before looking at his brother. "I think so. Randi was very hurt by something that happened between us in college. I think we've moved beyond that. As long as I don't do anything to break her trust, we'll be fine."

Dex nodded in agreement.

The rest of the morning was spent playing with Tripper, cutting a broken branch off the Red Maple in the front yard, and working up a small garden area along the edge of the driveway.

The butterflies in Davie's stomach had formed squadrons and were dive-bombing his guts by the time he and Dex were dressed in their western suit coats and starched Wranglers.

Dex insisted on driving Davie's truck, and that was probably a good thing. Even though it wasn't far from Randi's house to the ranch, his boot tapped a fast beat on the floorboard. "Can't you drive a little faster?"

"I swear, if you ask me that again, I'm going to slow down." Dex had taken the long way to the ranch, insisting they needed to top off the tank even though Davie had filled it the day before. Then, once again at Dex's insistence, they stopped at the convenience store for a package of cookies for the reception.

"This is total nonsense." Davie was on the verge of walking the rest of the way. "There will be more food there than an army could eat in a fortnight."

"Just doing as I'm told. You wouldn't want Mavis to be mad at me, would you?"

"Yes!" More mind games from the peanut gallery.

Davie leaned back in the seat and closed his eyes, but images of Randi naked, smiling, teasing popped up in vivid color. Jerking himself upright, he noticed they were almost home.

They drove past Lucy's house and on up the hill to the new home Dex had built for Mavis last year. An ivy and rose covered arbor stood in a corner of the large lawn. White folding chairs were arranged in rows and long strings of tiny, white lights had been strung from the porch to various small trees.

"Looks good," Dex said as he headed for his porch. "Come on in. Mavis made a big pitcher of lemonade from Nana Lucy's recipe yesterday."

"I think I'll go find Randi." Davie turned and started down the hill to the old ranch house.

Dex stepped in front of him, putting his hand on Davie's chest. "The whole purpose of this was to keep you apart before the wedding. I can guarantee you I'd have much rather spent the night with my wife in my own home."

Davie tried to step around his brother, but Dex got in his way again. Although he was almost four inches taller than his brother, he knew it would be a hard fought battle to get past Dex.

"Are you afraid if she has too much time to think she'll call the whole thing off?"

Davie scuffed the toe of his boot in the dust. "Kind of."

"Well, she won't. That woman is in love with you, and she's not going anywhere without you. Come on. Lemonade will make you feel better."

Drew came out of the house, a beer in his hand. "Need my help, Dex?"

Davie turned to his middle brother and frowned. "What's up with the beer? You don't drink."

"I do now. Come on in."

Davie gave up and followed his brothers into the house. "The only thing that will make me feel better is to have this over with. My gut keeps telling me something isn't right. Got something stronger to mix with that?"

"Can you imagine what my life would be like if I let you get drunk before your wedding? Randi, Mavis, and Nana Lucy would be lined up to kick my butt. Now take your Lemonade out to the porch and be a good boy."

They sank into the handmade Adirondack chairs lined up along the front of the house. The original ranch house had been built almost a century ago, by necessity in the draw near water. When Dex had looked for a site to build a house, he picked one with a view of sprawling pastures and the mountains in the distance.

Drew cleared his throat. "Chelsey can't make it."

"Kind of late notice, isn't it?" Dex put his glass on the table and glared at Drew. He glanced at his phone. "How are we supposed to find a replacement a half hour before the ceremony?"

"She was supposed to be here at ten this morning. She called an hour ago and said her flight was delayed." Drew drained the bottle and stood. "I need another one of these."

"What's going on with them?" Davie watched as Drew hurried through the door.

"The same old thing, but I think Drew has about had enough." Dex took another swallow of the lemonade and shook his head. "This is your day. We'll worry about Drew later."

Davie let his gaze wander over the landscape and soaked up the view of the ranch where he'd grown up. "Do you think Randi and I can make this work?" Somewhere in the depths of his heart, he had a horrible fear this was all going to go south. And watching his steady-eddy brother fall apart didn't help.

Dex punched him in the shoulder. "Got pre-wedding nerves?"

"I gotta admit I'll feel better when the preacher says we're man and wife."

CHAPTER TEN

Randi had been so nervous during the preparations for the wedding that it was almost disconcerting to feel absolutely calm. It had taken her long enough to figure out that marrying Davie was the right thing to do, But today she had no doubts.

As Randi stood from where Christina had applied her make-up, she caught sight of herself in the mirror. Having never been a girly-girl, she almost didn't recognize the elegant bride staring back. There was only one thing wrong.

Her sisters had done her hair into an elaborate up-do, but Christina had applied more eye makeup than she'd ever worn in her life. "You've got to take some of this off."

Christina stopped in the act of stowing her makeup into a custom-made case and grabbed Randi's hands. "Don't you touch that! You're beautiful."

Even her bossy younger sister couldn't put a dent in Randi's newfound tranquility. She kept her voice low as she worked her hands loose. "Come on, Tina. I look like a raccoon. Smokey eye just doesn't work for me. I don't want to walk down the aisle and scare my future husband."

Randi pulled a handful of tissues out of the box.

In a well-rehearsed mom move, Camille snatched the tissues out of her hand. "Let me do it."

"Camille, she looks great." Christina stood with her hands on her hips, the pointy toe of her expensive heels tapping out her exasperation. "And we're running out of time. The wedding is scheduled to start in ten minutes."

"It's her wedding, Christina. Let her do something her way for once." Camille applied makeup remover to one of the tissues and dabbed at Randi's eyes.

Randi watched as a rare smile spread across her older sister's face. "Besides, what are they going to do if she's late? Call off the wedding?"

As Camille finished reapplying Randi's eye makeup, Mavis hurried in, holding little Hailey's hand.

"Hi, Aunt Randi. You look pretty." Dressed in a frilly princess outfit and cowboy boots, it was obvious Hailey had chosen her own outfit for the wedding. "I'm so glad you're marrying Davie 'cause he's gonna buy me a pony."

Randi pulled her niece into a hug. "Can I tell you a secret?" When Hailey nodded, she continued. "He's going to buy me a pony, too."

"You two are incorrigible." Camille grinned and moved toward her daughter.

"I always wanted to be a flower grill." Hailey twirled away from her mother. "And now I am."

"That's girl, honey, not grill." Camille caught her daughter's hand just before she danced into Christina.

Hailey looked up at her mother. "That's what I said."

"You've got to admire a grill who knows what she wants." Mavis stepped around Hailey and walked to Randi. "The guests are seated. The minister is here, and Davie's about to have a meltdown. Are you ready?"

Randi's laugh was filled with happiness. "He's nervous. I didn't think Cool Hand Davie ever worried about anything." She slipped her feet into the strappy sandals Christina had loaned her then smoothed the skirt of her sleek wedding dress.

Randi knew how Hailey felt. She was a fairytale princess at least for today.

Mavis positioned the beaded headband and short veil into her hair, and gave her the once over before Christina pushed her out the door.

Dex sat on a freshly washed four-wheeler covered with roses, ivy, and lace. His gaze automatically went his wife first then it shifted to Randi. "Never thought I'd see the day when someone would give my wife a run for her money in the pretty department, but you are a close second."

Randi whispered in her almost brother-in-law's ear as she gave him a hug. "Thanks, I think."

The women helped her onto the back of the machine then followed them up the hill in Lucy's car. As they went in the back door of Mavis' house, Randi caught a glimpse of Davie before Drew hustled him out the front.

The sounds of the wedding march echoed through the house. She peeked out the picture window and saw all her friends and family and most importantly, Davie standing by the minister.

And the cameras.

Cameras were everywhere—cameras on tripods on either side of the minister, cameras on wheels moving up and down the aisle, and men with handheld cameras wandering everywhere. One of the show's directors and Mr. Hughes, who very wisely opted to deal with Christina instead of the happy couple, moved everyone into position.

Mavis and Christina each gave Randi a hug then Mavis took Hailey's hand. "Remember, when I tell you, you drop the petals on the ground."

Hailey clutched the basket to her chest and shook her head. "But, I like them."

Camille knelt beside her daughter. "I have a bag of petals in the car and as soon as Aunt Randi is married, I'll get them for you. Okay?"

The little girl nodded, gave Randi a hug around the knees, and took Mavis' hand. When Mavis and Hailey had made it half way to the alter Christina flashed a quick grin at her sister and stepped out the door.

Their father had died when Randi was thirteen. Dear old mom had escaped the responsibility of motherhood the day Camille had turned eighteen. When it came time to choose someone to walk her down the aisle, Randi chose her older sister. Camille was as close to a parent as she'd ever had.

Camille took her hand. "I'm so happy for you. Let's go get you married."

Randi was pretty sure she hadn't flown to Davie, but she couldn't remember walking a step. The minister might as well have been talking gibberish. Afterward she only remembered one sentence. "Do you take this man to be your lawfully wedded husband?"

She floated through most of the ceremony, but when Davie took her hand and slipped the big diamond engagement ring off her finger, she was confused.

He looked into her eyes. "With this ring, I thee wed." When he pulled a ring out of his pocket, she couldn't stop the gasp.

The rose gold of the band at first glance looked like copper. A tear-shaped turquoise stone was surrounded on one side by small diamonds. It was the most unusual wedding ring she'd ever seen, and she loved it.

She looked around the small group of friends and saw tears in Mavis' eyes and wide smiles on her sisters' faces.

"Before I pronounce you man and wife, there is one more formality." The minister's brows pulled down into a frown, and his lips thinned. When he glanced at Mr. Hughes, the man waved him on. He shook his head, hesitating before continuing the service. "If there's anyone who knows why this couple should not be joined together in holy matrimony, let them speak now or forever hold their peace.

Randi had been looking into Davie's eyes, waiting for his kiss when the words hit her. She turned to the minister. They hadn't practiced this part.

Davie turned to look at the minister then he grinned. He leaned forward and whispered in her ear. "No one would—."

A shrill voice came from the crowd. "I object." A pretty brunette with a young baby worked her way out of the seating and made her way to the front. "When I got pregnant, you said you'd marry me, Davie. You said you were excited to be a daddy."

Davie looked like he'd grabbed a live electrical wire. His eyes were wide. Shaking his head in denial, he reached for Randi.

Randi backed out of his reach. If he'd lied when she asked him about having a baby with someone else, what else had he lied about? She fled down the aisle toward the house, followed by Mavis and her sisters.

Davie's voice echoed in her ears. "Randi! Randi!"

"Lock the door. I need to think." Randi tore off the veil and hiked her dress up so she could pace.

The front door rattled as Davie pounded. "Randi let me in. That baby is not mine."

She walked over and laid her head against the door. "So you don't know her?" Her heart raced waiting for the answer.

"Yes, I know her, but you've got to believe me. That isn't my child."

Randi stumbled over to the sofa and sank into its plush cushions. She couldn't even do getting married right.

Every person on the guest list was a close friend or family, and now they'd all witnessed her downfall, but that wasn't the worst part. "Oh, god! Everyone in America will see this."

"Oh, honey. Maybe we can get them to cut that part out." Mavis laid her hand on Randi's shoulder.

She shook off her friend. Kind words wouldn't make this situation better. During all the times her brain had made up terrible scenarios of what could go wrong at the wedding, nothing had been as bad as this.

How was she going to move to where no one knew her without a job or the money from this show?

As she sat with her head in her hands, a thought wiggled its way into her brain.

The little whisper became louder and more insistent, and she knew it was the truth. Davie had never lied to her.

He's never lied to me.

After repeating the mantra silently several more times, she said it out loud. "Davie's never lied to me." She looked at the other women in the room. "He's done some stupid things, made some senseless remarks, and infuriated me more than once, but he has never lied."

But she'd lied to him about losing the baby. She hadn't told the truth, and it had cost her everything.

She'd lost six years with the man she loved because they hadn't been honest with each other. If a she didn't learn from her past mistakes, she'd be doomed to repeat them, and repeating the last six years was something she would avoid at all costs.

Jumping to her feet, she ran to the door, her skirt hiked up to mid-thigh. The right side of the up-do collapsed along her face, and she didn't care. "I'm getting married."

"That's our Randi." Mavis cried, heading out after her.

As the four women raced down the aisle, most of the guests stood, either in honor of the bride or to get a better view of what was going to happen next. Randi was pretty sure it was the last one.

She threw herself into Davie's arms.

"That's not—" Davie's voice broke.

"I know. You don't lie to me." She turned to the guests and shifted her gaze until she found the woman and baby. "I don't know who you are, but the game's up. Davie doesn't lie."

She turned back to the minister. "Pronounce us man and wife, or we'll find someone else to do it."

The minister shot Mr. Hughes a dirty look then smiled at Davie. "Young man, you're married. You'd better kiss your bride before she takes it out on all of us."

#

Not willing to let Randi out of his sight for even a minute, Davie followed her into the house. He hung his jacket in the closet and slipped into a pale green western shirt.

Randi changed into pressed jeans and a lacy shirt. Just the sight of her made his heart race, but then this woman would look good in a paper bag.

Her silver shoes lay on the floor where she'd kicked them off, and he bent and picked up one of them. "I love the look of these. Maybe we can bring them with us on our honeymoon." Davie lounged against the wall, watching his bride, twirling the shoe around his index finger.

His bride. He'd begun to think this would never happen.

She held a shiny white sandal in one hand and inspected the impossibly high heel. "They are pretty, but they kill my feet to even walk across the room."

"For what I have in mind, you won't be walking."

She gathered the other shoe off the floor and slipped them on her feet. As she stood, she tilted her foot back and forth, catching the glimmers of shine from beneath her pants. "How do you like them with my jeans?"

"I like them with everything or with nothing." Davie picked up the crumpled veil and laid it across the bed then he stalked toward her, wrapping her up and holding her close.

"I can't breathe." She leaned back just far enough to kiss him. "That's better." Her smile faded as she watched him. "What's wrong?"

"I didn't think you'd come back after that woman crashed the wedding." He let go of her and dropped to the bed. "Why did you?"

She sat beside him. "Once before, we didn't listen to each other. It ended in disaster. I promised myself I'd never do that again." She took his hand in hers and wove her fingers through his. "When you said that wasn't your child, I believed you. I'll always believe you."

Davie laid her back on the bed and kissed her. She finally pulled away, panting. "If we aren't careful, they'll come looking for us, and in about another five seconds, they'll get an eyeful. Let's go talk to our guests so we can make a quick getaway."

Friends had moved round tables onto the lawn and repositioned the chairs. As Randi and Davie came out onto the porch, a cheer went up, and Dex popped the cork on the first of many bottles of champagne. Women scurried around filling several large tables with food. One large galvanized stock tank was filled with beer and another one filled with soda.

Randi had taken the first sip of champagne when she saw Mr. Hughes working his way toward them, a camera crew on his heels. "Oh, shit. Here he comes."

"Be nice. We'll only have to see him once a month for the next six months then we're done with this whole mess." Davie put his arm around her shoulders.

"Well, that went well, don't you think? We have some great footage, especially when you stormed out, Randi." He waved the camera crew closer. "Now I need to ask you a few final questions. Also, Tommy here will accompany you on your honeymoon to get some candid shots."

They'd known someone would be around to film, and Tommy was the best of the bunch.

"How fortunate it was for you that the baby-mama showed up at the right time," Randi said, keeping her voice steady. "For a few minutes, I wondered how she found us, but then I realized anyone who knew Davie would know about the ranch."

"She didn't." Davie said, his voice flat.

Randi turned to her new husband. "She didn't know about the ranch or the wedding?"

"Either. I only dated her a couple of times. I never even told her I was from Oregon."

They both turned to Mr. Hughes.

"Well, about that. We needed a little more drama. Drama equals better ratings." Hughes self-satisfied grin told her all she needed to know.

"You brought her here?" Out of the corner of her eye, Randi saw Tommy giving her a nod.

Hughes' grin widened. "Good thing everything worked out for the best. I'd hate to have ruined your wedding, but either way would have worked out for us. We try to work a little surprise into every ceremony. If you'd left, we'd have had great footage anyway. The viewers actually like it when the couple splits up, especially at the ceremony."

Heat rushed through Randi's body as anger burned through her mind, but she managed to keep a smile on her face. "All's well that ends well, I guess. Davie, we'd better say our good-byes."

As she turned, she caught one of her stiletto heels in the turf and fell toward Hughes. She reached out her hands as if he could catch her, but the not-so-gentle push she gave the man sent him straight into the ice and pop filled galvanized tub.

Davie caught her and pulled her upright as everyone else stared at the man flopping around.

Tommy kept on filming. With a smile, he glanced at Randi and Davie. "He keeps telling me we can't have too much film. I'll send you a copy of this for your wedding memories."

Davie took her hand and pulled her away from the people trying to fish Hughes out of the tub.

She noticed none of those helpful people were her family. They stood back, their arms crossed, smiling.

When they'd reached the porch, Davie wrapped her in his arms. "Great fake back there."

Randi slipped out of her heels and dangled one in front of Davie's face. "You are the one who talked me into wearing these dangerous things. I can't help it if I tripped. If I'd fallen to my right, I might have hurt Hailey."

"But you could have fallen in with him."

"I was willing to take one for the team." She twirled the shoe around her finger.

"That's my cowgirl." They walked into the house, and Davie picked up the travel bag he'd packed earlier. "I don't suppose you found out where they're sending us on our honeymoon?"

"No, why?"

"Because after that stunt, Hughes might send us to Siberia."

Randi couldn't control her very unladylike snort. "That's no problem. I hear they have yaks there, and yaks are kind of like cows with big horns, and what do we do with horned cattle?"

He took her hands and pulled her close. Together they smiled and shouted. "We rope 'em!"

Romance Beneath A Rodeo Moon

If you enjoyed reading Winning A Cowgirl's Love, you can find Dex and Mavis' story in Book 1 of my Rodeo Road Series, Changing A Cowboy's Tune.

Changing A Cowboy's Tune-

When her fiancé demands Mavis abandon her goal of barrel racing at the National Finals Rodeo, she chooses to follow her dream and loses the man she adores. Dex wants nothing more than to marry the woman he loves and build a future on his family's ranch, but when he pushes her to settle into life as a mother and rancher's wife, she bolts. Years apart haven't dampened their desire, but can they see past their own dreams for the future and invent a life they both love?

https://amzn.to/2IwLrPH

Changing A Cowboy's Tune Excerpt

Her brows drew together and her jaw tightened, but with her heart shaped face, it was nearly impossible for her to give him a death glare. She reminded him of an angry Snow White in jeans and cowboy boots.

He turned on his charm. "Can we call a truce? Go back to being friends? We'll be seeing each other on the streets, and I'd hate to feel like I had to watch my back every second."

She looked at him for a minute then the corners of her mouth turned up. She smiled wryly and shook her head.

"You find that funny?" he asked, running their brief conversation through his mind. Nope. Nothing funny there.

Reaching through the open door, she held out her hand.

He took it in his, her skin soft and warm. This was more like it. He'd never had a problem talking Mavis into forgiving him.

Within seconds, she pulled her hand from his grasp, all

trace of humor gone from her expression. "I'll agree to a truce, but not friendship. I've had all the friendship from you I can handle in this lifetime."

Mavis had changed, become harder. No, not hard. More determined, less forgiving. It appeared her soft spot for him had disappeared.

"So we're non-friends, but not enemies?" He could work with this. Five minutes with this woman and he realized what he'd been missing. He reached for her hand again, and she tucked it beneath her thigh.

When she tilted her head, her thick hair fell across the side of her face. Flicking it behind one ear, she looked at him from beneath her lashes. "You remember the old saying, hold your friends close and your enemies closer? I want to make it perfectly clear. We're not doing that!"

Get to know the cowboys and cowgirls of East Hope, Oregon in the Sugar Coated Cowboys series. Begin with Cary and Micah's story in *Gimme Some Sugar*.

Gimme Some Sugar-

Pastry chef, Cary Crockett, is on the run. Pursued by a loan shark bent on retrieving gambling debts owed him by her deadbeat ex-boyfriend, she finds the perfect hiding place at the remote Circle W Ranch. More at home with city life, cupcakes and croissants than beef, beans and bacon, she has to convince ranch owner Micah West she's up to the job of feeding his hired hands. The overwhelming attraction she feels toward him was nowhere in the job description.

Micah West has a big problem. The camp-cook on his central Oregon ranch has up and quit without notice, and his crew of hungry cowboys is about to mutiny. He agrees to hire Cary on a temporary basis, just until he finds the right man to fill the job. Maintaining a hands-off policy toward his sexy new cook becomes tougher than managing

a herd of disgruntled wranglers.
http://amzn.to/1UDCemK

Gimme Some Sugar Excerpt

Snapping his head up, he whirled around, almost elbowing the woman standing behind him. Pulling in a deep, slow breath, partly to gather some semblance of calm and partly to adjust to the tingle where her hand met his arm, he took a step back before speaking.

"Help me with what?" Did he know her? He was sure he didn't, but man….

"I'm sorry. I didn't mean to eavesdrop, but I heard you say you're looking for a cook." Golden eyes the color of whiskey stared into his. "I cook."

He let his gaze wander over her, liking what he saw. She wasn't a local. Her white blond hair was as short as a man's on the sides and curled longer on the top and back. He hadn't seen any woman, or anyone at all who wore their hair like this. Of course, tastes of the people of East Hope ran to the conservative.

Despite the severe hairstyle, she was pretty. Beyond pretty. Leather pants showed off her soft curves, miniature combat boots encased her small feet and a tight tank top enhanced her breasts.

When she cleared her throat, he jerked his eyes up to her face. "It won't do you any good to talk to my breasts. Like most women, it's my brain that answers questions."

A smart ass and she'd caught him red-handed. His cheeks warmed. Damn it, he was blushing. This woman was not at all what he needed. Time to end this. "I have a ranch, the Circle W. We need a camp cook. A man."

Her eyes narrowed, and her body tensed. "It looks like you need any kind of cook you can get." She held her hand out, indicating the empty café. "Not a lot of takers."

She had him there. His gut told him he was going to regret this, but she was right. He had no choice. "I'll hire you week to week." When she nodded, he continued. "I've

117

got seven ranch hands. You'll cook breakfast and dinner and pack lunches, Monday through Friday and serve Sunday dinner to the hands who are back by six o'clock."

She bounced on the toes of her feet until she noticed him watching her then she pulled on a cloak of calm indifference. "You won't regret this."

He felt a smile touch the corners of his mouth as his gut twisted. "I already do."

http://amzn.to/1UDCemK

Come Visit Copper Mills, Arizona--a small town with a heart as big as the wide-open spaces and a long history of making dreams come true.

Silver Dreams…On a Tin Can Budget

She's found her dream… He's losing his…

Reed is desperate to save the family ranch and can't afford to be distracted by a fun-loving blonde who delights in making him laugh. But Catie is determined to leave tragedy behind her and reach for her dreams—no matter what. Working with silver and gemstones calls to her creative soul, and so does the quiet cowboy with a lot on his mind.

Can love bridge the gap between their two worlds?

Join Reed and Catie in this "opposites attract" cowboy romance where city meets country and sparks fly.

Silver Dreams Excerpt:

Reed watched as Catie's eyes went wide. Softer looking than her twin, but alike in every other way. His heartbeat picked up, and he almost reached out and pulled her into his arms.

"Is there anything else I can help you with, Mr. McCoy?"

Her voice changed from determined to that of a giggly high school girl in a scant second, and she batted her lashes fast enough to take flight.

He studied her for a moment longer. How could two women look exactly alike and give off such different vibes?

From what he'd seen of Eleanor so far, she was self-sufficient and studious, calm and contemplative. Totally focused on her new business. From what he'd heard, she succeeded in anything she undertook.

Catie appeared to be a little girl lost. The corners of her full, pink lips quivered as he stared, and he pulled himself from his musings. If she giggled one more time, he was out of here.

There was nothing about this woman that was what he was looking for. Catie was not the woman for him. There was no way he was going to be a caretaker to another person as long as he lived.

"Never mind. I'll talk to Eleanor later. Good luck with those beads." Now, why in the hell did he say that? Keeping his eyes on anything but Catie's pretty face, he turned and walked out the door. Once in his truck, relief covered him like a blanket.

Too bad it was immediately replaced by disappointment.

Eleanor Kershner was the type of woman he'd always been attracted to, but when he closed his eyes, it was Catie he saw. Catie's sweet expression. Catie's tempting body. Catie's wicked grin. After talking to her today, he couldn't imagine why people couldn't tell them apart.

He slapped his palms against the steering wheel. It must be the stress of worrying about the ranch that was messing with his mind.

A movement caught his eye, and he looked up to see Eleanor striding down the wooden walkway the town had restored in front of the shops in the original part of town. It didn't take a genius to know which twin was walking toward him. Eleanor's no nonsense walk ate up the distance from her car to the antique store. So different from the fluid way Catie moved.

There his traitorous mind went again.

It was time for him to find a wife and start a family, and Catie wasn't right for either position. That would be Eleanor.

Eleanor would have the business sense to help him regain ownership of the family ranch his father had pissed away. And the confidence to not be needy.

Babysitting dear old Dad, when the man finally gave up any pretense of work, had drained Reed.

Eleanor's smile was so small he wasn't sure her lips had moved after all. It occurred to him that he'd never seen her smile. He hadn't seen her show much expression at all as opposed to Catie whose thoughts played across her face in Technicolor.

Just as he reached Eleanor, Catie came through the door of the Turquoise Moon. "Ellie, did you get the mail? Did my package come?"

Reed shook his head. She was like a kid at Christmas.

He stepped in between the sisters and faced Eleanor. It was a boorish move, but he didn't have time to wait around while Catie got whatever bright bauble she'd ordered. "Do you have a minute?"

He felt a soft tap on his shoulder and heard the whispered word. "Ass!" When he turned to answer, he found Catie wearing the same smile she'd had in the shop, bright and sappy.

He suspected it was the one she bestowed on her few customers and on jerks. To give her credit, he had been rude, but still… "Excuse me?"

"Oh." She giggled after the word, but there was no humor in her gaze. "You are definitely excused. Now, Eleanor, if you'll hand me my order, I'll leave you to take care of Mr. McCoy all alone. He has something really important to discuss, and he's made it clear it would be over my silly little head."

http://bit.ly/SilverDreams

Fall in Love with the first book in the Change of Heart Cowboys Series: Radio Rose

She listens to crazies . . .
It's her job . . .
Late nights on the radio . . .

Most nights were typical. She does wonder about the callers, though. Still, it pays the bills, and she likes the work. The coffee wasn't so bad, either. The solitary routine of a radio talk show host was perfect for her, but that was all about to change.

A middle of the night car crash and a blow to the head has her wondering . . .

Is her savior one of the aliens her callers talk about or her ideal man?

The station is in trouble. Along with her small town.

The man from the crash has offered to help, but what's his agenda? There's something he's not telling her.

Can she trust him?

Funny, almost sweet, and a little snarky.
Radio Rose is a quirky romantic comedy you won't be able to put down. Get your copy today!

Radio Rose Excerpt:

Rose was still in shock and shook her head. What a mistake! Glass shards of pain sliced into her brain. She slammed her eyes shut and sucked in a breath.

The alien-repellant helmet slipped to the side, and he gently lifted it off her head. Pressing it into her hands, he waited for her to open her eyes.

She peeked at her helmet and saw half the lights had burned out. "Damn, piece of shit helmet. This piece of crap is guaranteed for ten years. How am I going to make good on the guarantee if I'm abducted? Answer me that."

"Are you dizzy?" he asked. "Can you walk?"

As she lifted her gaze to his eyes, firefly sparkles flashed across her vision. She'd forgotten he was there.

I must be out of my mind. Abducted by aliens, and I'm worrying about this piece of junk.

As she tried to answer, the words froze into little clumps of ice and melted back down her throat.

"How many fingers do you see?" he asked, holding up one hand.

"Hold them still so I can count."

"How many?" he asked again, impatience riding on each word.

It seemed a stupid question for an alien to ask, but now was not the time to question these guys on their mathematical skills. Focusing her eyes, she counted the fingers slowly, twice then told the truth. "Eleven."

"You need to sit down while I try to get you out of here." He carried her to a vehicle, opened the door and placed her on the seat.

"Don't take me with you. Please, I'm not a normal human. I wouldn't make a good specimen," Rose pleaded as she stuffed her trembling hands between her knees to hide the shaking. "Really, I'll skew your results."

She focused her vision and concentrated on his features. Nothing was making sense. He looked like a human, a darn nice one, but her callers had told her aliens could change form at will.

He placed her helmet in her lap. Only a light, here and there, was blinking now. Forty-nine dollars and ninety-nine cents down the drain when she didn't have money to spare. If she disappeared into outer space to be experimented on money would be the least of her worries.

She didn't have the energy to fight him when he lifted her legs, put them in the spaceship and dug around until he found the straps to tie her down. He reached across her, belted her in and shut the door. Now she was trapped. Running her fingers over the door, she tried to find the handle. Before she could make her move, she felt the spaceship lifting off.

***

"I'm Adam Cameron. I was there when you wrecked your car last night, and I brought you into the hospital. I wanted to come by and see how you were doing."

Her eyes didn't blink, and she didn't move.

"Do you remember anything?"

"Not much." She peeked at him from under her lashes then her eyes widened, and she gasped. "But I remember you. You're one of them." She pulled the sheet up to her eyes and peered out at him. "No, that can't be right, because there aren't any of them are there?"

The nurse had told him the diagnosis was a concussion, but this sounded more like full on, raging paranoia.

For the first time Adam really looked at her. There were dark smudges under her coffee brown eyes. Even her olive skin was pale. A large purple lump stood out on her forehead, partly hidden behind her glossy, black bangs.

"Wait, why were you there?" Rose's voice was a hoarse whisper. She lowered the sheet an inch.

"My rental car broke down, and I was stranded on the side of the road. I couldn't get any cell reception to call a tow truck. I tried to flag you down to see if I could get a ride."

Incomprehension faded from her eyes as understanding moved in. "It was just you." Rose released a sigh as understanding dawned on her face. "I remember now, and it was just you."

"Yes, I . . ."

A blush warmed her face as she cut him off with a slight wave of her hand. "You stepped out into the road and waved your arms. You were dressed in black."

"Yeah, that was me," he said, his attention drawn to her pretty pink cheeks.

"And?"

His eyes snapped up to meet hers. "I thought you'd see me sooner. I'm sorry. I didn't mean for you to get hurt."

"You scared the bejeezus out of me. I don't know when I've ever been so petrified. What an idiot."

"Hey, I said I was sorry," Adam took a step back and reminded himself she was hurt. People in pain sometimes said things they didn't mean. Before he could apologize again, she spoke.

"I'm not calling you an idiot. Although one of the first things we learned in kindergarten was to wear light colors after dark." She paused for a minute, closed her eyes and massaged her temples with her fingertips.

"I'm calling myself an idiot for believing the crazies I talk to all night. I must have hit my head pretty hard, because when I came to, I thought you were an alien. Wow, every awful thing I've heard on my show came rushing back to me." She raised her eyes to meet his as she dropped her hands to her lap. "Like I said, what an idiot."

"What show?" he asked.

"I'm Radio Rose. I host a late night talk show. Most of my programs are on alien abductions."
http://bit.ly/RadioRose

ABOUT THE AUTHOR

Stephanie Berget was born loving horses, a ranch kid trapped in a city girl's body. It took her twelve years to convince her parents she needed a horse of her own. She found her way to rodeo when she married her own, hot cowboy. She and the Bronc Rider traveled throughout the Northwest while she ran barrels and her cowboy rode bucking horses. She started writing to put a realistic view of rodeo and ranching into western romance. Stephanie and her husband live on a farm, located along the Oregon/Idaho border. They raise hay, horses and cattle, with the help of Dizzy Dottie, the Border Collie and Cisco, barrel and team roping horse extraordinaire.

Stephanie is delighted to hear from readers. Reach her at
http://www.stephanieberget.com
Facebook:
https://www.facebook.com/stephaniebergetwrites/
Amazon: Stephanie Berget
Twitter: https://twitter.com/StephanieBerget

Made in United States
North Haven, CT
25 January 2022